ISBN: 978-0-578-44148-1

Thank you to everyone who supported me.

FINDING THEON

The Traveler Book One

JORDAN
KELLEY

Table of Contents

Chapter 1

Chapter 2

Chapter 3

Chapter 4

Chapter 5

Chapter 6

Chapter 7

Chapter 8

Chapter 9

Chapter 10

Chapter 11

Chapter 12

Chapter 13

Chapter 14

Chapter 15

Chapter 16

Chapter 17

Chapter 18

Chapter 19

Chapter 20

Chapter 21

Chapter 22

Chapter 23

Chapter 24

Chapter 25

Chapter 26

Chapter 27

Chapter 28

Chapter 1

I landed with slightly bent knees, glad to see I was finally getting the hang of this. Dusting off the sand, I sighed, relieved to be out of that desert. If I never had to see endless miles of sand again, I would be a happy soul.

I looked up at the only source of light; a large white dome in the center of the ceiling casting a shadowy light on the circular room. It was a stark contrast to where I had been, making me shiver at the slightly eerie feel. It was no wonder I never spent much time here in this eternal night.

I searched for Long Feather and found him standing beside his basin of water which served as a window to the outside world.

Long Feather commented, "You had a rough one."

Sending him a look, I replied, "You did drop me in the middle of the desert, miles from my assignment, without a drop of water."

He shrugged. "Transporting people is not a perfect art form; you know that."

I didn't respond since I knew he was not remorseful about it. I looked at him and noted how normal he seemed. Sure, he wore robes instead of modernday clothes, but at first glance, he didn't seem the "I see and know all" type. Then again, on closer inspection, you couldn't overlook his deep, otherworldly eyes. They made you feel like your very soul had been laid bare for all the world to see.

It still made me shiver after being around him for nearly ten years.

Shaking out the last of the sand from my clothes onto the perfectly clean stone floor, I walked up to him. "Can I see her?"

He frowned but nodded. "Yes." He waved his hand over the water, moving it into small ripples until an image formed. I smiled. My sister was carrying on a lively conversation with two other girls around her age. She showed no signs of the rare illness that had nearly claimed her life years ago. "There's no chance it will come back?"

Long Feather shook his head. "Not as long as I live. That was the bargain."

With a sad smile, I continued watching them laugh and talk with animated expressions. What would they say if they saw me now? I was a far cry from the seventeen-year-old girl who had disappeared eight years ago. Instead of toting around my current book, I was carrying a bow and arrows, along with a few traveling necessities in a satchel. I didn't have a single thing from home, just the distant memories.

"Hello?"

Jarred out of my thoughts, I snapped, "What?"

He eyed me suspiciously. "I have the next planet picked out. It is very similar to yours, but not as enlightened."

With a skeptical tone, I asked, "What does that mean?"

"It is of the horse-drawn carriage variety."

I rolled my eyes. "Great. Is this a just-discovered-electricity kind of place, or a King Arthur still rules the land type?"

He smiled. "More of a bow and arrows time frame. You will fit right in."

I scoffed. "Who needs help this time?"

He waved his hand over the water, bringing a new image into view. Five men on horseback rode in a line down a dirt road through the woods. The first, a tall, broad-shouldered man with dark, sun-tanned skin. Next, a tall but lean man with light, brown hair, and an alert expression followed. Third, was a short, muscular man with dark hair who seemed to be expecting trouble. Following him, a young man who looked to be a slimmer and much more relaxed version rode with an almost carefree expression. Lastly, a dark-haired, green-eyed rider who seemed to be tenser than the others, brought up the end of the line. From the looks of them, I had already missed some of the excitement, but then, I was never called when things were going smoothly.

Long Feather said, "The ruler of Carp has gone missing, and as a result, things are quickly falling apart. I need you to keep Prince Alton here alive. There are many trials ahead for his people, and they will need him in the days to come. Find Theon, if you can. He will balance things out again."

"And if I cannot find him?"

Long Feather turned with a grave expression.

"Then you will have a lot more to deal with before things are back on track."

Focusing back on the riders, I wondered why Long Feather had picked this time and place to meddle in. He always had a reason, even if he didn't tell me what that reason was.

He handed me a sealed letter. "Give this to King Charles, he will recognize the seal, and not question your motives for being there."

I took the letter and stashed it in my satchel. "Anything else I should know?"

"Well, there is one thing."

"Yes?"

He drew in a deep breath. "The men decided to go on a hunt. Unfortunately, they are going to run into more trouble than they are prepared for. You had better be off."

I sent him a glare just as the now-familiar tingling sensation started. I braced as everything sped away in a blur. I fell into the white tunnel, trying not to turn upside down. Shielding my eyes with my hands, I hoped I didn't land on my head.

Chapter 2

The bright light was replaced with sunlight as I landed feet first on the ground with a sense of relief.

Straightening, I loosened the grip on my bow while taking in my surroundings. The trees smelled earthy under a beautiful blue sky, making me wonder if this was such a bad place after all.

Looking around, I wondered which way I should go. Long Feather seemed to enjoy making me figure things out rather than send me where I was needed. Spotting movement, I tensed, turning to see a flutter of wings. Surprised, I realized it was a blue butterfly only; it was about a foot across. Stepping closer, I watched it bob its black-tipped wings in a lazy rhythm, drifting down the trail. Glancing both ways, I decided it was fifty-fifty, and started after the giant-winged creature. Content to follow its path, I jerked as a hair-raising roar rent the air in the opposite direction. Reminded of my reason for being here, I ran towards the shouts and horse's shrill screams. They were close, but I feared not close enough. What if the prince died before I reached them? Remembering the last person I had failed to save, I ran faster, determined to find them.

Rounding the corner, I slid to a stop as what appeared to be a very large prehistoric tiger tackled a man off his horse.

The muscular one shouted "Luke!"

The remaining riders attempted to charge after it, but the terrified horses wouldn't go near it.

Notching an arrow, I aimed for the torso of the tiger, and quickly released it. The arrow landed just behind its shoulder, but too high off the mark. The animal roared, spinning away from the young man, turning to me. I notched another arrow, aiming for its chest as it began racing towards me on pounding feet.

Releasing the arrow, I started to feel real panic when it only tripped as the arrow stabbed into the orange fur, then scrambled up and kept running.

The men, unable to make the horses go forward, leaped off their horses, going in pursuit of the animal on foot.

I quickly released another arrow, hitting the base of its neck as the tiger seemingly unhindered, closed the last few feet between us. I ducked but not fast enough, and it reached out, slapping me to the ground with a large paw.

Retrieving my short sword from my belt, I only had time to block its teeth as it lunged for me. Its mouth snapped closed around the blade, and I held it with both hands, feeling the steel cut into my left hand.

The green-eyed one with a sword drawn shot forward, stabbing the animal in the side. It let out a startled sound, before dropping dead on top of me. Light and sound suddenly snuffed out, and I froze.

Realizing I couldn't breathe, I pushed against the dead weight, but it barely budged. Now safe from being eaten, I feared I might be smothered instead. "Hold on milady!" someone said.

It took what seemed hours, but eventually, the massive beast was dragged off me. I sucked in a deep breath, relieved to see the sun again.

Five sets of eyes stared down at me. The one with a dark complexion and a kind look reached forward, offering his hand.

I let him help me up, then glanced at the massive animal. "What do you call them?"

Luke replied, "We call them cats."

"Of course."

Looking at each of them, I was surprised to see that they were all right. Even Luke, who had been tackled, seemed well enough.

The man who had been the lead rider stepped forward, now with a distinct air of authority. "You have been injured, my lady."

I followed his brown-eyed gaze to see four long cuts wrapping around my arm. I frowned. Those would be one of the more notable scars I had received.

"Allow me." He tore his shirt sleeve and, at my nod, moved forward to tie it securely to my arm.

The other four watched me with suspicion, no doubt wondering about my strange clothing. If their medieval clothes were any indication, my boots, fitted pants, and a loose shirt belted at the waist were not exactly common here.

The brown-eyed man asked, "May I inquire as to how you became alone out here, my lady?"

I started to retrieve the letter but paused when the other four tensed. Slowly pulling it out of my satchel, I handed it to him. "I have been sent to protect Prince Alton while things are ... uncertain."

He inspected the seal on the letter, seeming suspicious, then said, "This is familiar."

The brown-haired man asked, "May I?"

The prince handed it to him, and he said, "This is Joseph's seal."

The muscular one asked, "Why would he send someone without giving us prior notice?"

I replied, "With all the trouble you've had, he wanted me here as soon as possible."

They seemed distrustful, but the Prince took the letter back and handed it to me. "Your search has ended because you have found me."

I smiled politely, ignoring the look of interest on his face and the disapproval from the others. Stepping carefully around them, I began retrieving my arrows. "Then it is a good thing I ran into you when I did."

He nodded. "We had planned for a deer hunt, but it seems we will not have such luck today."

The one with light brown hair cleared his throat. "We should return, sire. The King will send out a search party before too long."

Prince Alton nodded again, this time with a look

of resignation. "We cannot have that now, can we?" He turned to the younger man. "Luke, gather the horses."

Disheveled, and still looking a little rattled, Luke ran off after the scattered horses.

The prince asked, "Do you have a horse as well, my lady?"

I shook my head. "I came on foot."

He pondered that a second before saying, "You will ride with Sharrow then."

The green-eyed one who had finished off the tiger glanced at me with surprise but didn't argue.

Luke came back, leading four horses and allowing the fifth to follow at a distance. Prince Alton strode forward and swung up onto his horse with practiced grace.

I followed Sharrow to a large black charger and reluctantly swung up behind him.

Prince Alton gathered his reins, ready to leave. "We will have your injury seen to, and sort out everything at the castle. I am sure my father will wish to read the letter first."

"Of course."

We started forward, and I shifted, trying to find a less uncomfortable position behind the saddle.

The Prince asked, "Have you traveled far, my lady?"

"Yes, I came from across the sea, and you needn't call me my lady. I have no such aspirations. Most just call me The Traveler."

Surprised, he said, "Such frankness is a rare thing.

But if that is what you wish, I will call you Traveler."

Relieved he didn't question my vague answers, I simply replied, "Thank you."

He said, "You must forgive my manners. I have yet to introduce everyone. The man to your right is Sir Thomas." Pointing to the youngest man, he said, "This is Luke, and behind you is Luke's older brother, Sir Henry."

I acknowledged each, receiving a cautious look from Thomas, a smile from Luke, and a curt nod from Henry.

Sir Thomas said, "We should hurry, the lady will need tending to, and we have been gone longer than is advisable."

In answer, Alton cued for a canter.

Sharrow glanced over his shoulder. "Hold onto me, milady. My charger is fast but not the smoothest."

I nodded and loosely wrapped one arm around Sharrow's waist while keeping the other protectively tucked in. Truth be told, I had forgotten it entirely, knowing it would heal by tomorrow morning. But I could not very well say that in an era where I was likely to be burned at the stake for healing that fast.

We didn't slow for what seemed miles, and I hoped my next assignment would be set in another century. I had gotten the hang of archery and swordsmanship, but I feared horses would be the one thing I would never master.

Taking the opportunity to study the small group, I started making a mental list. I noted that Sir Thomas was cautious, and from what I could see, just as fiercely loyal to Prince Alton as the others. If it came down to a fight, I would want him in my corner. Henry, on the other hand, I couldn't read as well. He was quiet and stern, making me wonder if I could trust him beyond protecting the prince. I suppose he had a similar opinion of me though. Shaking off the unsettling feeling, I turned my thoughts towards Prince Alton. He seemed young and inexperienced as a leader, but with guidance from the others, I doubted there was a problem they could not overcome. At least I hoped so. He turned looking at me, and I looked forward again, having been caught staring. Sharrow glanced over his shoulder asking, "Do you fare well, milady?"

"Yes, I am fine."

He turned towards the road again, but not before I could see the concern in his eyes. I could tell him that the wounds were already beginning to heal and would be fine come tomorrow, but not wanting to be taken for a witch, I remained silent.

I faced ahead to see that the road had opened, revealing the tower of a castle in the distance. No matter how many times I saw one, they never failed to impress me. It would likely be here hundreds of years from now, a testament to the uncounted numbers who had built it. I wondered what I would find ahead and if I would be able to figure out who was trustworthy in time. That was always the trouble with these kinds of assignments; everyone thinks they can do a better job than the person in charge. I just had to keep Alton alive long enough to find out who presented the biggest threat.

Chapter 3

As we traveled farther down the road, the woods gave way, revealing a better view of the castle. It was surrounded by smaller buildings from what I could see, and beyond that stood a great stone wall encasing everything. Even from here, I could faintly smell the ocean and hear the rumblings of a thriving city.

Alton looked over at me, saying, "Welcome to The Southern Kingdom."

I replied, "It's amazing."

Sharrow asked, "Have you never been this far south, milady?"

Raising my voice to be heard over the horse's hooves, I replied, "No, I haven't had the chance."

Henry looked at me with suspicion but didn't comment. I hoped it wouldn't prove to be a problem later on. It certainly wouldn't be the first time someone made things harder by distrusting me.

It seemed we were going to ride straight into the castle as we raced along the dirt road only slowing when we reached the main gates. A few animals spooked, but from the unsurprised looks on the guards, I assumed it was a common habit.

Now at a more comfortable pace, we rode through the gates, wading into the crowd as the sounds and smells washed over me. The people upon recognizing the prince bowed their heads and stepped to the side, letting us pass. At least I wouldn't have to worry about his people being a threat to him. As loyal as they seemed though, I could feel a tension in the air that didn't belong. Did they know trouble was coming? They all seemed to be going about their daily tasks, but there was a certain briskness to it.

Sharrow turned slightly in the saddle saying, "Not long now."

I nodded then realized he couldn't see it. Glancing at my arm, I could tell it had stopped bleeding but still had a faint burning sensation. I might have to keep a wrap on it for appearance's sake just until it is forgotten by the others.

We approached the castle gate which also hosted a portcullis, making me wonder if it was to keep people in or out.

A single guard posted nearby nodded to Alton who asked, "Did I miss anything?"

The man shook his head and replied, "Not from what I can see, your highness."

Satisfied with the answer, Alton led the way inside, stopping halfway into the courtyard. He dismounted, and a boy came running up to take his horse. Sharrow stopped his horse just past the gate and realizing I still had my arm around him, let go and swung off hastily.

He dismounted gracefully and turning to me asked, "Are you alright, milady?"

I smiled and replied, "Yes I'm fine, thank you."

I could tell he didn't believe me, but he didn't press it further.

Alton walked up as our horses were being led away and said, "Once you have been tended to, I will find my father, and you can give him the letter."

I replied, "If it is alright with you, I would rather have the introductions first, and I am to stay at your side night and day until I am recalled."

He raised an eyebrow, and Luke asked, "Night and day? We do not even spend that much time with him."

Henry frowned and Sharrow offered, "I think she should be looked after first. Then we can sort out the rest."

Thomas added, "I would feel better if we knew the truth of it first."

Alton looked at me and asked, "If you can wait a short while?"

I nodded, and he said, "Luke go find my father and tell him to meet us in his study."

Luke glanced at me, looking displeased at being sent off again then left. I noticed a few people look our way as they passed but no one approached.

Alton said, "This way."

I followed, flanked by Henry on my left and Sharrow on my right with Thomas behind. It made me feel a little boxed in, but I didn't blame them for being careful, especially since for all they knew I might still be a spy.

People moved to the side as we walked, briefly acknowledging the prince and for no reason, I could see cutting a wide path around Sharrow. He didn't seem to notice it, but it would be impossible not to. There must be some history I didn't know about. Determined to find out later, I looked into the doorways of the rooms and halls we passed, trying to memorize the layout. This place was a maze to me, but Alton led the way without any trouble, later coming to a stop at a wooden door. The guard close by opened the door without a word, then moved back to his post. Alton thanked him and went inside. I paused after taking two steps in and could only stare at the floor to ceiling bookshelves filled to the point that some of the books sat precariously on the edge of their shelf. A large desk sat a few feet away, covered on one half by stacks of paper while the other half was covered with maps. A large, dark-colored chair sat empty behind it matching the other various chairs placed around the room. It struck me as the kind of place where one might seek refuge from the chaos of the outside world.

Sir Thomas took a seat by the door, while the others shuffled around, looking for a place to sit. Spotting one by a window, I picked up the books lying there, and not knowing where they went, simply sat down placing them in my lap. A man walked into the room resembling Alton, and everyone got up again.

I stood still holding the books, and the man seeing this said, "Please sit. I am told you have had an eventful day."

Luke walked in saying, "That is one way of putting it."

I sat, grateful to be off my feet and said, "Thank you."

He nodded and seemed surprisingly hospitable. He wore the clothes of a modest nobleman, not the flashy attire I might have expected after seeing such a large castle. What gave him away was his air of authority. It showed in the strict set of his shoulders and his silent but purposeful stride. I doubted he could be mistaken for a commoner even if he wore an empty feed sack.

Alton said, "Father, our guest has a letter for you."

The king walked over to me and trying not to drop the stack of books; I handed him the letter. Moving to the desk, he slid some papers back and leaning on it, opened the letter. The others busied themselves glancing around the room, while Alton watched his father no doubt searching for a clue of what the letter said.

After a moment, the King announced, "Your help is most welcome, Traveler. Joseph speaks highly of you, which is a rare thing indeed."

I just nodded, knowing I had never met this Joseph and if I was lucky, never would.

Alton asked, "He is one of our largest trading partners correct?"

The King nodded saying, "Yes and as such he has a large stake in keeping our kingdom intact. No one else would pay the prices we do for the lavish goods he sells." The king continued saying, "Alton will see to it you are tended to and a place near his quarters prepared for your sleeping arrangements."

I stood placing the books back in the chair and said, "Thank you."

He added, "Should you require anything at all, you need only ask."

I nodded, and a man rushed into the room saying, "My apologies your highness, but your presence is needed in the main hall."

The king nodded, then looking at Alton said, "The council meeting is this evening, and it would be best if you were there as well."

Alton replied, "Of course, father."

The king left without another word, already turning his thoughts to the next task at hand.

Alton instructed, "Henry, would you see that she has a room readied across from mine?"

Henry still looking like he wanted to personally kick me out of the castle, nodded saying, "Consider it done."

He glanced at me then left.

We all walked into the hallway, and Alton asked, "Sharrow if you could take her to get her arm looked at and Thomas, Luke, I need your help getting everything ready for tonight. The council meetings are always chaotic, and I would like to smooth it out as much as possible beforehand."

Sharrow replied, "We will find you afterward."

I was reluctant to leave Alton, but I knew Thomas was a capable swordsman.

We started to part ways when I stopped suddenly

and looked down the hallway making everyone pause.

Alton started to speak when a little boy came running up to Sir Thomas taking his hand and pleading, "Father, come quickly!"

Sir Thomas asked, "What is it, son?"

The boy responded in a rush, saying, "Mother, she's sick. I saw it. She said not to bother you, but I knew you would want to know."

Alton said, "Go on Thomas, I will have my physician sent to your room shortly."

Thomas said a quick thank you and left, having picked up the boy so he could walk faster.

Alton turned to me and asked, "How did you know something was wrong? I did not hear him call out."

I replied, "I can sense when you or those closest to you are in danger."

He asked, "From how far away?"

I shrugged saying, "Distance doesn't matter. The link will last until I am recalled."

Luke said, "Next, you are going to say you can fly."

Responding in kind, I said, "Sadly no, I cannot fly."

Sharrow asked, "Can you tell what ails Thomas's wife?"

I shook my head saying "No, but it isn't too serious. That much I can tell."

Alton said, "I am glad to hear it." Then looking at my bandaged arm said, "I will not delay you any further, Traveler. Come find me afterward. I would like to discuss this ability of yours in more detail."

I replied, "Yes, your highness."

He took his leave much as his father had, and Luke took a moment to look me up and down before going. Now they definitely thought I was a witch.

Sharrow said, "Come, I will show you the way."

I fell into step with him, wondering how I was going to explain this one. Somehow, I didn't think they would believe that I was sent here by someone they knew as a mythical creature. Maybe I would get lucky and he would forget about it.

Chapter 4

We came to a small room where an older man sat reading a large leather bound book that looked old as the castle walls.

He glanced up and asked, "How can I be of service?" Then seeing me, he ushered, "Come sit here."

Taking the chair he had occupied, I said, "I just need a new dressing on it."

He started unwrapping the old bandage and said, "It seems to be healing well. I would imagine it will be back to normal in a week or so."

Sharrow glanced over surprised but kept silent. I didn't comment since I knew it would be good as new minus the scar by tomorrow.

He turned looking into a back room, and called "Peter!"

I heard a shuffling noise, then a young man maybe fifteen years old, came in and looked at Sharrow and I before walking up to the physician and saying, "Yes?"

The older man instructed, "Go find her a new shirt and some bandages."

Peter took off like a shot, and the physician stiffly said, "You may wait outside, sir."

Sharrow ignored the dismissal and replied, "The prince has asked that you attend to Sir Thomas's wife as well. Her son said she was sick."

At his nod, Sharrow looked at me, then went out

into the hall shutting the door behind him.

Even more curious now, I looked at the disgruntled man, and he said, "Begging your pardon, milady, but why are you with the Eirian? He might be one of the prince's closest friends, but he is still one of them."

I asked, "What makes you say that?"

He replied, "His eyes of course. Only those with Eirian blood have green eyes. Did you not know that, milady?"

I shook my head saying, "No, I am not familiar with the history here."

He started to reply when Peter came back with a bundle of fabric.

He set everything down, and the physician began cleaning around the cuts on my arm while he said, "The short version of the story is, the Eirian people tried to take the castle not so long ago I might add, but we were able to send them running back home. Both sides lost more men than the history books could ever record, and many still regard those with green eyes as the enemy. Mark my words, milady; trouble follows an Eirian no matter who his friends are."

I frowned wanting to stand up for Sharrow somehow, but the truth was I knew very little about him. So I didn't say a word and busied myself with looking at the bare room. Everything in it served a practical function down to the plain wooden chair beside the bookcase and the two beds with brown blankets on them. The floors were also bare, making the room feel cold. It wasn't the kind of place I would want to stay in if I ever really needed medical help.

Finally, he finished, and getting up I said, "I'll just use the back room to change then."

He backed a step, letting me pass and said, "Of course, milady."

Taking the white shirt similar to mine, I went into the back room and closed the door.

Stepping into the hallway again, I saw Sharrow leaning on the wall watching people with his dark green eyes. He didn't seem sinister even dressed in solid black just aware of his surroundings.

Then he spotted me and walked over saying, "We should see if Henry has finished clearing a room for you, so you do not have to carry all your things everywhere."

I didn't like the idea of parting with my things, especially since most of them were from another time but it would look strange to carry my bow and arrows all over the castle, so I replied, "Alright."

He assured, "There is no need to worry, milady; no one will take your belongings. All the rooms have doors that lock."

I asked, "Why do you call me milady instead of Traveler like the others?"

We began walking as the physician and Peter left going the other way, and Sharrow replied, "Because I was taught to always address a lady as such, even if she is not high born."

I added, "Even if she wears riding breeches?"

He smiled as we rounded a corner and replied, "Even then."

I wanted to ask how he had become so close to the royal family if he was an Eirian but that might lead to questions about my origins, something I wasn't going to try and explain if I didn't have to.

We nearly ran into Henry a short time later as he was coming out of a room, and in a rush, he demanded, "Did you take a long way around? The meeting has already started, and he will be expecting her there."

I looked at Sharrow who said, "I thought we would take a back way and avoid-"

Henry cut in saying, "It does not matter now. Here, give me your extra belongings my lady and Sharrow can take you to the meeting."

I gave him my bow and arrows along with my satchel, and he took them disappearing into a room and swiftly locking the door before handing me the large iron key.

I thanked him, and he nodded, still looking uncertain of me as Sharrow said, "We better hurry, milady."

I nodded, and he led the way down a larger hallway that was so busy I felt as though I was attempting to swim upriver.

He finally slowed when we came to a closed door where several guards stood posted.

Sharrow said, "Prince Alton is waiting for her."

They stepped aside; some looked at me with distrust while others were more curious.

Sharrow said, "This is where we part ways, milady."

I asked, "You're not going inside?"

He shook his head saying, "Only the king, his son, and a few council members are allowed, unless you are invited."

I nodded feeling strangely uncomfortable at being sent in alone and turned, opening the door and going inside. Taking a moment to adjust to the dimmer lighting, I spotted the prince sitting beside his father towards the end of the table. The conversation came to an abrupt halt, and everyone looked over at me.

Alton broke the silence saying, "She is my guest."

The nearly dozen men also sitting at the table were uncomfortable with this idea, but didn't oppose him. He stood and pulled out a chair beside him waiting for me to enter the room. Not wanting to bring any more attention to myself, I crossed the room and took the offered seat. Choosing to avoid the glances, I looked instead at the map on the table. Covering it were numerous cities and villages, the names elegantly written out beside a black dot marking its place. I noticed worn places on the corners of the paper where the rocks sat to weigh it down and over some of the cities surrounding the Southern Kingdom like they had been pointed to repeatedly.

Around me, the conversation picked up again

slowly at first but growing louder as men argued with one another about their land, loyalty, and responsibilities. It wasn't long before they forgot about me altogether, and I was grateful. It gave me the chance to listen to each one without worrying they were editing what they were saying for my sake.

Suddenly, a Lord across from me dressed in armor stabbed his finger down on the map north of the Southern Kingdom shouting, "If Carp gives their ships to Eirian, they will lay waste to my entire keep before doing the same to your kingdom!"

The King chided, "Lord Wesley, kindly take your seat."

Embarrassed, he did sit down, but still looked angry enough to spit.

The King said, "Do not think I will forsake you or yours when you need help most. I have not forgotten that you sided with me when the Eirian people attacked last."

Lord Wesley replied, "My apologies, your grace; I forget myself sometimes."

The King said, "Everyone is feeling a little anxious."

A middle-aged man wearing a flowing brown robe asked, "Are we certain they intend to take the castle? It has scarcely been more than twenty years since the last attack."

A man who had been silent up until now replied, "Every indication has pointed to that explanation. Why else would Carp give their ships away?

With control of the Southern Kingdom, Fredrick would own the entire eastern side of the country, along with the overseas trading routes."

Prince Alton asked, "Have you heard anything about Fredrick's uncle?"

The man turned his light blue eyes to the prince saying, "All I could find out was that he suddenly went missing, and now Fredrick has the throne. There are rumors Theon is being kept at Eirian."

Remembering that Long Feather had told me to find Theon, I leaned forward listening intently.

Alton asked, "Would it be possible to send a search party for him?"

The blue-eyed man shrugged and said, "You could send them, but they would not likely return. No one who has been to Eirian has ever returned since the war."

The King reasoned, "But if he were found, it would put a stop to Eirian's attack. It would take too long for them to march this far south without the ships."

The blue-eyed man said, "I could have a search party ready by tomorrow."

A voice from the far end of the table asked, "And what about Carp's ships? They will set out any day now."

The man wearing a brown robe said, "Someone needs to speak with Fredrick and try to change his mind about this. He is young and rash, but surely some sense can be talked into him."

The King said, "We have already tried talking him

out of it. He denies any plans of an attack or the alliance with Eirian."

Lord Wesley demanded, "Then take an army! A good show of force would convince him of his folly."

Alton asked, "What if I were to go?"

The room went silent, and everyone looked at him like they just realized he was even there.

He added, "That would show him we are serious about stopping this before it becomes a real conflict."

Lord Wesley said, "I still say you should take a few thousand men. My keep is close enough that you would have an impressive escort."

The blue-eyed man countered, "Or he would hear of the troop coming his way and send his soldiers south while his ships go north."

Alton said, "I agree. I cannot take what appears to be a fighting force to his front door."

The King asked, "You are certain about this?"

Alton nodded and said, "Maybe I can talk him out of it. I think we owe our people that much before we ask them to put on their armor once again."

The room was silent a moment before the King said, "Then take a handful of men and leave at first light. Fletcher, do you have someone who could serve as a guide?"

The blue-eyed man nodded and said, "Yes, I have just the man in mind. He is familiar with both Carp and the people who will know more about what is going on."

The King nodded and said, "Good, it is settled then. In the meantime, we will prepare for the worst, just in case. Even if Fredrick gives up on this pursuit, we may still have to deal with Eirian."

He stood, and everyone rose as well.

Looking around at all of us, the King said, "Thank you for your time. I realize there is very little of it to go around."

Everyone responded respectfully, then started filing out.

Alton turned to his father and said, "I will not let you down."

The King smiled sadly and clasping Alton's shoulder said, "I know, son." Then looking at me said, "Keep him safe."

I replied, "I swear it on my life."

He replied, "I will hold you to it."

Alton glanced back at me then said, "I will take Thomas and the others as well."

The King said, "You better let them know, so they have time to prepare."

Alton led the way out saying, "First, I need to see about Thomas' wife. I could not ask him to leave her if she needs him."

I didn't respond. I just followed him out, thinking about all the cities we would need to pass through to reach Carp in one piece. I was beginning to understand why Long Feather thought Alton would need me to survive this.

Chapter 5

I stepped into the hallway and realized it was now dark. All the commotion had slowed down to just a few people coming and going. The guards looked tired, making me wonder how long we had been inside.

Alton asked, "Sharrow, is something wrong?"

I turned and saw him leaning against a wall facing the guards. He looked calm but silently alert.

He replied, "I was anxious to find out what decision would be made."

Alton said, "Come, walk with me."

Sharrow straightened, glanced at me, then fell into step with Alton who led the way. I followed at a distance, not sensing an immediate danger and wanting to give them some space.

They talked amongst themselves, planning the trip I assumed, and since I didn't know the names of most of the cities, I decided they didn't need my help on this one.

A short time later, Alton stopped and knocked on a closed door. Sharrow looked over at me like he wanted to ask something but didn't.

The door opened, and Sir Thomas came out asking, "Did you hear the news?"

Alton shook his head saying "No, what did the physician say?"

Thomas exclaimed, "I am going to have another son!"

We were all momentarily taken aback, then Sharrow and Alton congratulated Thomas whole heartily.

I heard a soft voice from inside the room ask, "Who is that, Thomas?"

He turned, saying "Apologies, I did not mean to wake you. I will just be out in the hall."

He carefully closed the door and stepped a few feet away saying, "Can you believe it?"

Alton smiled and said, "I can indeed, brother. It is wonderful news."

Thomas's joyous expression melted to one of concern, and he said, "I can see in your eyes that something is wrong. What happened at the council meeting?"

He looked at me for the first time then back to Alton, waiting for an answer.

Instead, Sharrow replied, "Alton is riding out in the morning for Carp."

Thomas said, "I can be ready by then."

Alton replied, "No, you should stay here with your wife. This is going to be a dangerous trip and-"

Thomas cut in saying, "Where you go, I go. Lana knows that, and it will be months before the baby comes."

The Prince admitted, "I would prefer all of you to be there as well."

Thomas replied, "Of course, who else is going to keep this bunch in line?"

Alton smiled and said, "We need to find Henry and Luke. Father has also asked Fletcher to provide us with a guide who will meet us at sunrise."

Thomas frowned and said, "I do not trust Fletcher. There is something about him that unsettles me."

I had felt the same way the first time I saw him, but I hadn't sensed danger towards the prince from Fletcher, and that's all I could worry about for the time being.

Alton argued, "He has never given us reason to doubt him, and we need a guide. My name will only go so far. We need to know who's who and how to get out of the city if things go wrong."

Thomas agreed reluctantly, and Sharrow said, "We should find Luke and Henry, then discuss it."

Alton said, "It is late, they may have retired to their rooms by now."

Sharrow replied, "You know Luke is still likely out on the town. I have not seen him since this afternoon."

Thomas said, "Henry will know."

We started walking again, this time with Thomas in the lead and Alton in the middle while I was in the back. They seemed to have gotten used to me shadowing them everywhere, but I guess if you lived here, having people around all the time was normal, expected even.

Sharrow dropped back even with me and asked, "How are you faring, milady?"

I replied, "Fine, it's been a whirlwind of a day, but I think I'm keeping up."

Alton praised, "She has been very resilient. Sometimes I think I would rather be on a battlefield than in the council meetings."

Thomas added, "They are a kind of battlefield. Just not the kind where you can see an attack coming."

Sharrow replied, "I agree, it is better to see your opponent's move than try and wade through the politics of his speech."

Alton groaned, saying, "You are making me weary just talking about it."

Thomas replied, "Agreed, enough of politics for one day."

We came around a corner, and I got a sudden chill, causing me to stop dead in my tracks.

Sharrow, seeing this, called, "Wait!"

Everyone stopped, and I ran towards the prince as a blur suddenly dropped from a rafter in the ceiling above him. Thomas reached for his sword which wasn't there, and I saw the man wielding a dagger lunge as I slid between him and the prince, bringing my arm up in an attempt to block the attack. The silent man was faster though, and I could only watch as his blade sunk with terrible accuracy into my chest. Thomas grabbed the man, yanking him away as Alton caught me from behind, trying to pull us both out of the way but too late. Sharrow helped Thomas subdue the assassin in a matter of seconds, and I looked at the source of the pain radiating in my chest only barely aware of a distant scream and Alton lowering me to the ground. I looked at the hilt with disbelief, and a loud voice spoke shaking me out of the shock.

Alton who was bent down beside me with a horrified expression said, "Hold on Traveler, help is coming."

I turned seeing the assassin unconscious on the floor and said, "Should have known sooner."

Alton sounding a little rattled admonished, "Never mind him, you just focus on me."

I focused instead on the blade inches from my heart and rasped, "Pull it out."

Alton shook his head saying, "No, you will bleed out if I do it now."

He started to pick me up, but I pushed him away saying, "Just pull it out. I will be fine."

He frowned, and someone took my hand, squeezing it tightly.

I was surprised to see Sharrow and pleaded, "You have to trust me. Take it out."

He didn't move for what seemed hours, then reached out and took the hilt in his hands.

Alton shouted, "No! You will kill her."

Sharrow replied, "She has been right so far."

I held my breath, and he pulled the dagger out, making me gasp.

Turning, I coughed up blood on the stone floor, and Sharrow asked, "Now what do I do?"

I coughed again and said, "Give me a minute."

He raised me up into a sitting position and tucked a few stray hairs away watching me intently.

Four guards came running up, and Alton stood saying, "Take him to the dungeons."

They looked over at us taking in the scene, then picked up the assassin and walked away.

Thomas said, "We should get her out of the hallway."

I looked to see a crowd forming but couldn't seem to gather my thoughts enough to worry about it. Sharrow picked me up, and I turned away from all the chaos, not realizing until now how weary I had been.

The next thing I knew I was being set down on a bed and looked up to see all five of them piled into the room with me. When had Henry and Luke appeared?

Sharrow sat in a chair beside the bed and Alton asked, "Can I get you anything?"

I shook my head a little uncomfortable with all the attention and replied, "No, I will be good as new tomorrow."

To prove my point, I pulled the tear in the fabric of my shirt showing the angry looking red skin already closing.

Luke said, "I do not believe it. What are you?"

I didn't know how to even begin that answer, but Sharrow came again to my rescue saying, "She is injured; that is what she is. Now leave her alone."

At his warning tone, Luke frowned but didn't say anything else.

Henry asked, "Does your father know?"

Alton answered, "Maybe someone told him in all the chaos. I need to speak with him though."

I started to sit up and pleaded, "Wait, he may not be the only one out there."

Sharrow laid his hand on my shoulder stopping

me and said, "Some of the king's guards have been assigned to Alton, he will be safe."

Relieved, I settled again with a cringe and Sharrow offered, "I will stay with her."

Alton nodded and said, "We may have to postpone the trip until after this is sorted out."

Thomas replied, "We may not have that much time."

Alton frowned but decided, "I will let you know after I speak to father."

Sharrow nodded, and they left their voices growing more distant until I couldn't hear them any longer.

Sharrow took my hand and asked, "Are you sure there is nothing more I can do?"

I shook my head saying, "It just needs time to heal."

He asked, "This is not the first time you have used yourself as a human shield, is it?"

I replied, "Sometimes there isn't enough time to do anything else. I should have known sooner."

He watched me a moment then said, "You were still able to save him, and he will not forget it. I would not be surprised if they named a wing of the castle after you."

I smiled and said, "I hope not. I'm not supposed to leave a big mark on history."

He asked, "Is that why you do not use your name?"

I nodded and wanting to steer the conversation in another direction said, "Thank you for staying with me."

He replied, "It is the least I could do."

I knew he felt guilty for not stopping the attack sooner, but I couldn't seem to find any words of comfort for him. This had been a close call, and everyone knew it. The only question was who sent the assassin to kill Alton?

Chapter 6

I woke and looked to see Sharrow asleep sitting in the chair beside the bed. He seemed so relaxed and unguarded I hardly recognized him. I was tempted to reach out and sweep back a lock of hair that had fallen across his face but thought better of it. Carefully pulling my hand from his, I stood up and rolled my shoulder. I was glad to find it had regained its full range of motion. My clothes, on the other hand, were not so lucky. I seemed to go through shirts faster than I could replace them.

Taking in the room, I spotted my bow and arrows beside a change of clothes on the table, accompanied by a single candle. It was nearly burned out, and I could hear several voices passing by on the other side of the closed door. What time was it? The room didn't have a window but guessing from the number of people walking around; it wasn't sunrise anymore. Had Alton left without me? I needed to change and find out.

Turning back to Sharrow, I stepped closer and lightly laid my hand on his arm saying, "Sharrow?" He woke instantly, his green eyes focusing on me with a surprised expression.

He jumped up, causing more of his short black hair to fall forward and asked, "Milady, why are you out of bed?"

I replied, "It's okay; the injury is as good as gone."

He looked at me skeptically, and I rolled my shoulder saying, "See?"

Relief washed over his features, and I asked, "What happened last night? Did Alton come back?"

He blinked, trying to keep up with my quick change of subject and replied, "Yes, we decided to wait until you were ready." Then looking at the low burning candle, he admitted, "I must have dozed off."

Opening the door and drawing curious looks from people passing by, I knew I had likely ruined whatever good reputation he might have had here.

Seemingly unaware of the onlookers, he said, "I will go see where everyone is and come back for you."

I replied, "Alright."

He started to leave, then looked back at me and said, "I do not know where you came from milady, but I am glad you came."

I smiled and replied, "So am I."

He left, softly closing the door behind him, and I couldn't help noticing how empty the room felt now.

Shortly after, a knock on the door made me pause and opening it; I saw a girl standing there holding a basin of water in both hands and a towel draped over her right arm.

She said, "He asked that I bring these to you, milady."

I stepped aside letting her pass and asked, "Who did?"

She set everything down on the table and replied,

"The prince's friend. The green-eyed one."

She did her best not to stare at all the blood on my clothes while saying this, and I didn't blame her for being confused. There was so much dried blood on my clothes she might even think me a ghost.

She asked, "Can I get anything else for you, milady?"

I replied, "Something to eat would be wonderful. I didn't get the chance before."

She replied, "Of course, milady."

I thanked her, and she nodded before going out and closing the door behind her. Walking over to the water, I found that it was warm and after locking the door, started the long process of scrubbing crimson out of my skin.

"Milady?"

Hearing Sharrow's voice, I quickly finished braiding my waist length black hair and replied, "Come in."

He opened the door slowly and seeing me smiled and asked, "Ready?"

I nodded and asked, "Where is everyone?"

He replied, "In the courtyard."

I asked, "They haven't been waiting on me all morning, have they?"

He replied, "No, Alton had his hands full dealing with the assassin."

Slinging on my satchel and making sure I had everything, I followed him out and asked, "Has he said anything?"

Sharrow frowned and replied, "Someone got to him last night, so all we have now is a body with no identifying evidence. The King nearly forbade Alton from leaving, but it was finally decided he needed to go now more than ever."

The fact that someone was going through so much trouble to get rid of Alton made me nervous about the trip, but maybe they were right in having him go ahead with the plan. I would want to know who was trying to kill me, even if I had to venture into danger to find out. The trouble with that was Alton had to be kept alive long enough to find out who the someone was.

Chapter 7

The mid-morning sun shone on my skin as I stepped outside and saw how busy the area was around us. Riders would come flying in on spent horses and leap off before running inside and leaving their sweat-drenched horses to the stable hands, while others went flying out at the same break-neck pace.

Looking around, I spotted Alton amid all the chaos, talking to a man a short distance away but when he saw us, he said something to the man, then picking through the crowd, came over to Sharrow and me.

A short distance away, Sir Thomas swung up onto his horse while Luke and Henry did the same. Alton now within earshot said, "I am very glad to see you have recovered, Traveler."

I replied, "Thank you."

He asked, "I assume Sharrow has filled you in on the night's events?"

I replied, "Yes, I was sorry to hear about the assassin."

He frowned and said, "It just makes it all the more important that this war is ended, soon." Then turning, he said, "Daniel, come and meet our Traveler."

The man Alton had been speaking to earlier, came forward and quickly looked me up and down before taking my hand and kissing the back of it and said, "It is a pleasure to meet you, milady."

He had such a charming smile I had no doubt ladies fell for those blue eyes that were a shade lighter than mine.

I, however, gently pulled my hand back saying, "Thank you, but please call me Traveler."

He smiled and replied, "Of course."

I noticed Sharrow's frown when Daniel had taken my hand and wondered why.

Thomas who was waiting nearby said, "We should go before we lose the daylight."

In answer, Alton motioned for a horse to be brought to me before swinging up onto his war charger and moving towards the gate. I looked at the large sorrel horse and thought here we go again.

Sir Thomas took the lead with Daniel and Alton while Henry and Luke were in the middle, leaving Sharrow and me in the back. I was farthest from the Prince, but from here I could keep an eye on everyone. We kept a quick pace, trying to make up for lost time which made conversation almost impossible. I didn't mind though. As much as traveling by horseback wasn't my favorite, it felt good to be on the move again. I had been doing this long enough that staying in one place just felt strange. I doubted if I, for some reason was allowed to go home, would be able to return to living a normal life. Somehow, a nine to five job didn't compare to helping a prince stabilize a country.

Alton slowed to a stop and said, "We are taking a short break."

We all dismounted and after seeing to my horse, I walked around, stretching my legs a bit.

Daniel came up to me and said, "I am told you appeared out of nowhere and saved the Prince."

I stared at him a moment trying to decide what to say and noticed a few of the others were listening. Daniel might be a charmer, but there was a hidden depth to him that made me feel defensive. Did he distrust me or was he just curious about his traveling companions?

I replied, "I was on my way to the castle when I heard the cat and soon after found the Prince's riding party."

He commented, "Well, I am sure everyone is glad you found him when you did."

I nodded, still unable to tell what his motives were and said, "Yes, it was good timing."

He seemed to ponder this a while then started to say something when Alton said, "Daniel, I would like to discuss our plans about Carp."

Daniel replied, "Of course, your grace."

He excused himself and walked towards Alton. I nodded to the Prince who gave me a look of understanding, then turned his attention to Daniel. I wasn't sure why he had intervened, but I was glad. My story was flimsy at best when everyone knew I was first seen too far west to have come from the ocean as I had told them.

Sir Thomas walked over to me and warned, "Be careful with Daniel, he is much sharper than he seems."

I nodded and replied, "Yes, I picked up on that as well."

Henry walked up and said, "He has a point. You did just appear."

Thomas replied, "I do not care if she came from the moon. She has proven herself trustworthy."

Henry frowned at me, and I decided I better sleep with one eye open on this trip.

Luke came over asking, "What is going on? Why do all of you look so serious?"

Henry said, "Nothing is going on. Come and help me with the horses, I think we are leaving."

I turned to see the Prince moving back towards his horse while still talking to Daniel and Sharrow. They seemed to agree about something, and shortly after Sharrow and Daniel went for their horses.

Facing Sir Thomas, I said, "Thank you."

He nodded and turning to leave said, "We owe you even if Henry does not agree."

I wanted to say that I would settle for not having to worry about being stabbed in the back.

On the road again, we took up the same places in the lineup.

Sharrow moved over closer to me and asked, "What was that about?"

I replied, "Not everyone is sure about me yet."

He frowned and asked, "Who? Daniel?"

I asked, "Why do you dislike him? Did something happen before I joined the group?"

He replied, "Daniel has many faces and a long trail of broken hearts behind him. I find it difficult to trust such a man."

I said, "But Fletcher picked him for this trip."

Sharrow replied, "No one knows Carp better, and I think he is loyal to the royal family, but beyond that, I do not know."

I asked, "What has been decided about Carp?"

Sharrow replied, "Daniel is going to arrange an audience with Fredrick while we stay outside of the city until it is safe for Alton."

Glancing ahead to make sure no one would overhear, I replied, "I am all for keeping the prince safe, but I don't like the idea of showing up after everyone knows he is here with little protection."

Sharrow said, "We decided it was better than parading him through the city. Especially since we do not know how he will be received."

After thinking on it, I decided they were probably right, and our not so merry little band could only protect Alton from so much. I asked, "What does he plan to do if Fredrick won't call off the attack?"

Sharrow frowned and said, "We will have to fight. If it comes to a battle, then the Eirians will have the upper hand. They outnumber us and have a much harsher way of living which has hardened them in ways that the people of the Southern Kingdom have not been."

My horse snorted suddenly, reminding me to pay

attention to him as well. Shifting a little in the saddle, I looked over at Sharrow and said, "But the Eirians attacked recently, and they were pushed back."

He nodded and said, "They came on foot, which cost them some of their numbers and gave us time to prepare the walls. We have enough supplies below the castle to last a year if necessary, but the ships might be a problem. They were unable to blast their way in last time, but with Carp's warships, they would have the means."

I glanced up at the sky wondering if I was going to be enough help to stop this war. Of course, Long Feather never said I was supposed to stop the war, only that I had to keep Alton alive.

"Milady?"

I turned to look at Sharrow and said, "Sorry, what were you saying?"

He replied, "I was asking if you knew how long you would be here. There is a good chance we will meet the Eirians head on, and we could use your help."

Reminded of my bargain with Long Feather, I replied, "I do not know. When I am called back, I won't have a choice but to go, no matter what is going on at the time."

He asked, "You do not do this out of free will then?"

I shook my head saying, "I owe a debt, so I go when and where I am called."

He asked, "Forgive my prying, but what kind of

debt would require such diligence?"

I looked ahead, making sure the others were not too close, then replied, "A favor was done for my family, so now I am in a kind of life-long service."

He asked, "Was this favor worth it?"

I nodded saying, "Yes, I would make the same choice again without a second thought."

He watched me a long moment not saying a word, even though I could see in his eyes that it was eating him alive not to ask more about it. I could have told him the whole story, but looking ahead at the group, I reminded myself that sooner or later I would be off to another place and likely never see any of them again. I couldn't get attached to people; it hurt too much, and I knew better.

Chapter 8

Sir Thomas led the way inside the small Inn while we followed in a single file, keeping the Prince in the middle of the group. He was covered with a plain brown hooded cloak and had removed his jewelry. One misstep would alert the entire building of his presence, something I hoped we would manage not to do.

A middle-aged man walked towards us, welcoming the group and asking if we would be staying for the night while I took in the room. It was built more for practicality's sake than anything else and stocked with worn wooden furniture, but it would provide a welcome break from the road and the constant looking over our shoulders for danger.

Thomas picked an empty table towards the back of the room, and we took a seat, with everyone trying to stay where they could see the comings and goings of those around us in the dimly lit room. There were only about a dozen others, and most were too drunk to recognize the Prince even if he had come in wearing his most formal attire. There were two couples however that looked to be spending the night here as well. They appeared to be nobles, and I wondered if they would be able to recognize Alton. Looking at Sharrow, I motioned to them, and he nodded slightly before whispering something to Thomas. Daniel glanced at the couple, then at me with a look of understanding before turning to Alton.

After a moment of talking it over, Sharrow instructed, "Henry, see that some dinner is brought up and the rest of you wait a little while before you leave. Thomas, Alton, and I are going upstairs."

Henry replied, "Agreed."

They left, drawing a few glances, but no one looked overly interested. Maybe things would go smoother now that we were out of the castle.

Now alone with Luke, Daniel, and Henry, I wished I had gone with the first group and not stayed here. The uncomfortable silence was so thick you could only cut it with a knife. Too bad I couldn't fix it that easily.

Luke broke the silence saying, "I say we draw straws for the second bed."

Henry smiled, and Daniel replied, "That sounds fair, but I am sure whoever the winner is will give that honor to our Traveler."

I replied, "Thank you, but I can sleep on the floor as well as anyone else."

Daniel replied, "Of course, but as knights and agents of the crown, we could not possibly allow such a transgression."

Henry rolled his eyes, and I was close to doing the same. The long line of broken hearts Sharrow had spoken of couldn't be that long if this was how Daniel went about wooing women.

I replied, "Maybe there won't even be a second

bed."

Luke commented, "Well, I am going to find out."

He got up having finished his dinner and without another word left.

Daniel asked, "What is bothering him?"

Henry shrugged, got up, and left as well.

Daniel turned to me and started to say something, but I stood up and said, "It has been a long day. I think I will go on up too."

He replied, "You are quite right, Traveler; it has been a long day."

Nodding, I started for the stairs and heard him catch up with me. Taking them two at a time, I quickly followed the faint voices and slowly opened the door, relieved to see that there was in fact only one bed and the Prince was sitting on it. The less special treatment I got, the easier it would be for people to forget I was ever here.

Everyone glanced over at us then went back to their unpacking in various places while Sharrow sent me a questioning look. He glanced behind me at Daniel with suspicion, then looked at me again. I shook my head slightly, and he frowned before looking away. With an inward sigh, I decided this was the most complicated trip I had ever been on, and that was saying something.

Picking a spot in the far corner under the only window, I laid out my things, knowing at least that I wouldn't get stepped on during the night.

Chapter 9

Opening my eyes, I saw Sharrow step into the hallway and slowly close the door behind him. Looking around, I was relieved to see that everyone else seemed to be asleep. Carefully going around everyone, I went out and spotted Sharrow at the top of the stairs. He paused as I closed the door, then glanced down into the quiet dining room below before walking over to me.

I asked, "What's wrong?"

He replied, "Nothing, I just felt restless and decided to step outside."

I watched him in the shadowy lighting and tried to decide if he was telling the truth.

After a moment, I replied, "Guess that makes two of us."

He nodded and motioned for me to take the lead. I walked downstairs glad it was deserted and went outside letting Sharrow close the door after us.

He commented, "We might get locked out."

I replied, "Our room has a window if need be."

He smiled then, and although I didn't want to ruin his mood I asked, "Why did you give me such a strange look earlier tonight?"

Sharrow replied, "I could tell something was off, but Luke did not say anything about it when he came up."

I replied, "It was awkward is all. The three of them are the most suspicious of me even now, and that made our dinner conversation short-lived."

Sharrow replied, "I can see their side of things, but I also saw you jump in front of a would-be assassin for the prince."

I just nodded and said, "There are always those that never believe my intentions to be good. My saving grace is that I never stay long."

He asked, "Where will you go after this?"

I shrugged and replied, "I won't know until just before I get there."

He asked, "Have you always traveled alone, milady?"

I nodded and hearing a noise, looked across the street but saw nothing out of the ordinary.

I added, "I'm used to it now."

He looked at me with those green eyes that seemed to see into my soul, making me look away suddenly.

I said, "I should go."

I turned to leave, but Sharrow said, "Wait, I did not mean to upset you."

With my hand on the door, I looked back and replied, "You didn't."

He didn't believe me but let it go at that. With a final glance, I went inside and berated myself for following him in the first place. He had a way of constantly reminding me how alone I was without ever trying to. I had to focus on the goal, and that didn't involve my personal feelings.

Closing the bedroom door, I went over to my things and quietly dropped onto the thin blanket separating me from the floor. I wondered when he would come back, then shook my head trying to focus on the task at hand.

Suddenly, I sat upright knowing in my gut that there was trouble coming, and Thomas asked, "What is it?"

I whispered, "Shh."

He quieted, but now the others were up and arming themselves. I peeked out the window and saw just a flicker of a shadow. Reaching for my bow, I notched an arrow and waited. I heard the others moving around and hoped the prince was out of the way. Feeling a chill, I scanned the area just as men appeared climbing onto the roof and heading for the window. I saw the moonlight's reflection on a blade and released my arrow.

A man shouted as he fell and Daniel beside me said, "There are too many. Out the front door!"

I let another arrow loose before dropping my bow and picking up my sword as men came towards us at a full run.

Looking back, I saw them lead Alton out while Henry shouted, "Where is Sharrow?"

I realized he must still be outside, and hoped he was unharmed. I hadn't sensed anything, so he must be alright, but where was he? Just then, men poured into the window pushing me back by pure force in numbers. I cut down the first two so fast that the others paused a second before regrouping and attacking again. Diving into the fray, I tried to keep anyone from getting past me, but there were just too many. There was shouting behind me, but in all the chaos I couldn't tell what was happening. Then hearing Henry shout "Back to the room!" I knew things were only getting worse. Ducking an attack, I sliced through a man off to the left while another tried to get past me on the right. Forced to back up, I looked back and saw Luke pushing the door closed while Alton wedged a chair under the knob. Turning back, I spun away from a knife on its downward arc and leaped back into the attackers now having some backup.

Thomas appeared at my side offering, "Some help perhaps?"

I barely had time to answer as two more came in the window, but were made to stay back when Henry jumped into the fight as well.

I shouted, "Sharrow?"

Thomas cut down a man with practiced ease and replied, "No one has seen him."

Worried now, I pushed through and finally made it to the window. Looking out as Henry and Thomas finished off the last of them, I spotted several horses lined up nearby. Then looking back to see that the prince was unharmed, I ran out and looked to see Sharrow astride his horse, holding the reins of the other horses.

He asked, "Milady?"

I replied, "We are alright!"

He warned, "Hurry, I see more coming!"

Turning, I ran back and grabbing my things said, "Sharrow is out front with the horses."

In mere seconds, we had all climbed out the window, and I heard the bedroom door being kicked in. Alton reached the edge of the roof first and dropped down before running for his horse, followed by the rest of us one at a time.

I waited on the roof sword drawn until everyone was ready and Sharrow shouted, "Jump!"

Not needing to be told twice, I jumped the ten feet and scrambling up, climbed onto my horse as the others took off. Looking back, I saw more men climbing onto the roof and shouting curses at us.

We rode hard with Daniel in the lead, Alton in the middle and Sharrow and I bringing up the rear. I thought we would ride clear into the next day, but after what seemed hours, Daniel slowed down, giving our dead-tired horses a break. I looked back but saw nothing out of place. It was still dark out, but there was a faint line of light starting to appear over the hill. It was just enough for me to see the stressed expressions on everyone's faces.

Alton asked, "Is anyone injured?"

Glancing at each member of the group, I saw that everyone had been a little roughed up but nothing serious.

Suddenly, Daniel asked, "May I speak with you, your highness?"

Alton looked surprised but said, "You can say it in front of the group."

Daniel was quiet a moment then turning asked, "Where were you, Sharrow?"

Before he could respond, Thomas angrily answered, "I will not have you questioning his loyalty."

Sharrow replied, "He has the right to ask. I went outside for some air and saw men going into the Inn. I tried to fight my way back inside, but I could not get past them, so I went for the horses."

Daniel said, "I understand that he has been a long-time friend, but he is still of their blood."

At that Sharrow bristled, but didn't say a word.

Alton ordered, "That is enough, Sharrow is not to blame. I will vouch for him myself."

Thomas, Henry, and Luke said the same.

Daniel replied, "You cannot blame me for pointing out the obvious."

Alton replied, "Perhaps not but it is wrong all the same."

Sharrow still hadn't said a word, and his face was a pure mask, making me wish I could tell what he was thinking.

Thomas said, "I think we should stay on the road from now on."

Daniel replied, "Agreed."

Alton said, "Good, now let us go before something else happens."

Daniel looked at Sharrow who only stared at him in return; then everyone started walking again.

I moved over closer to Sharrow and asked, "Are you alright?"

He nodded stiffly and said, "No matter how many years I spend here, I am still distrusted."

I replied, "I understand to some degree."

He looked at me then and his face cleared. He asked, "Why do you believe me? You know me the least."

I shrugged and said, "I can just tell."

He smiled faintly and said, "If only everyone else could too."

Chapter 10

Thomas sat down beside me with a heavy sigh saying, "I am getting too old for this."

I smiled in the dark and saw the amused but slightly exhausted look on his face in the firelight. He said, "Thank you again, for warning us of the attack at the Inn."

Remembering how close it had been, I replied, "I only wish I had known sooner."

He pointed out, "We escaped without losing anyone, so I would say it went better than expected."

Unable to disagree and knowing there was no point in berating myself further, I asked, "Could you tell where the men had come from?"

Thomas shook his head saying, "They were covered head to toe, and with the cover of the night might as well have been ghosts."

I frowned at the dirt, wishing I knew at least who was currently after us and asked, "How long will it take for us to reach Carp?"

He replied, "Not long, especially with the breakneck pace we were doing today. It might make for a rough few days ride, but maybe we will avoid whoever is chasing us."

Watching the empty road before us, I thought to myself if only we could be so lucky.

Looking over at Alton talking to the others with ease you only gain from years of friendship, I asked, "How is he doing?"

Thomas replied, "As well as anyone in his position could I think."

Reminded of the task ahead, I asked, "What is this new ruler of Carp like?"

He frowned and answered, "Young and rash. He was never meant to have the throne, and that is what must have inspired the takeover."

"What are our chances of talking him down?"

Thomas sadly replied, "Not good from what I know of him. Even if it is a wasted trip, we must find out more about what happened to his uncle. Theon being back on the throne will be the deciding factor in whether or not a war breaks out."

I nodded, knowing, either way, my job of keeping the prince safe was about to get a lot more difficult.

Sharrow walked over, handing a bowl of watered down stew to Thomas and me, then took a seat keeping everyone in his line of sight.

Thomas tilting his head towards Daniel and said, "You should not allow his false accusations to unsettle you. We all know you are no less loyal than any one of us. Even the King would say as much."

Sharrow nodded but still seemed upset about it. He looked at Thomas saying, "I barely even remember Eirian but I am still treated as an outsider, despite growing up in the castle."

Thomas assured, "I would change it if I could, Sharrow. To the four of us, you are family, but old resentments die hard for those who remember the war and all the chaos it created."

Sharrow replied, "I know, and I am grateful to have been accepted when I had no home and no one else to call family."

Thomas nodded and Sharrow looking frustrated said, "I should go and check on the horses."

He glanced at me, starting to say something, then turned and left. Once he had walked far enough away, I asked, "If you don't mind me asking, how did the five of you become friends?"

Thomas smiled and said, "I suppose we do seem an odd bunch."

I shrugged and said, "Not that strange."

He relented, "Perhaps not, but to answer your question, Henry's and my father are close friends of the king, so we spent most of our time at the castle. Luke, of course, being Henry's brother followed him everywhere we went, often getting into trouble for not staying at home, so eventually, he was allowed to tag along. As for Sharrow, we met under different circumstances."

Thomas frowned, appearing lost in his thoughts for a moment then continued with, "His people, the Eirians, do not allow their citizens to leave or anyone to enter their lands. However, when war broke out, some of the villagers took the opportunity to flee, and some escaped. However, most villagers like Sharrow's family were hunted down by their soldiers. Henry, Alton, and I were with the king's riding party when we found him as the lone survivor of an Eirian attack. He was sitting on the road holding his younger brother and refused to let anyone bury him, so Alton climbed off his horse and sat down beside him all afternoon, finally managing to talk Sharrow into letting go."

I looked over at Alton, deciding maybe Long Feather was right in saying that he would be a good ruler in the days to come.

Thomas added, "Ever since then, the five of us have stuck together through the years. Even after I married, the king saw to it that a room was set aside for my wife and me so we could remain at the castle."

Leaning back on my hands, I said, "I'm not sure what is more impressive, the story or the family that came to be because of it."

Thomas nodded saying, "Most do not know, but I think everyone will agree that you have earned some trust from us.

I smiled my thanks and Sharrow came back, sending a quick smile to me and a nod to Thomas before laying out his bedroll.

Thomas admitted, "I wish you were able to stay longer. I have never seen Sharrow light up quite like when he is around you."

Surprised, I sat up saying, "No, you must be mistaken."

He chuckled and said, "Anyone with eyes could tell you two are kindred souls."

Looking over at Sharrow with regret, I replied, "Even so, I must move on once everything is back to normal."

Thomas said, "Then know that you will always have a place here should you choose to return."

Turning to look at him, I replied, "Thank you."

He smiled, and standing said, "I bid you goodnight, Traveler."

I returned the gesture saying, "And you as well."

Later that night, I laid on my side listening to the others talk and staring up at the stars wondering if I would ever have a place to call home.

Chapter 11

"I will return as soon as I can."

Alton cautioned, "Be careful, Daniel."

He nodded and glanced at all of us once more, then slipped out of the room.

Luke dropped into one of the three chairs saying, "Now we wait."

Thomas peering out of the curtained window asked, "Are we certain about this place?"

Alton picked up a candle off the table and lit another brightening the room a little before saying, "Daniel says the owner of this house is a friend."

Henry asked, "So that means we should blindly trust him?"

Alton sat sword-in-hand saying, "We do not have many options here."

Sharrow commented, "It does not feel right."

I had to agree that waiting in this dark, cold house on Daniel's word alone did not sit well with me either, but Alton was right. What else could we do?

Luke added, "I say we just go there now and see what is going on."

Henry asked, "You would rush in throwing caution to the wind and risk all our lives?"

Luke frowned settling further into the chair saying, "It sounded better than just staying here."

Alton said, "All we can do right now is wait and see where things stand. Then we can decide from there."

Everyone agreed reluctantly, and I hoped we were making the right call.

A knock sounded on the door, making everyone jump. The door slowly opened, and a pleasant looking man stepped in saying, "Apologies, I thought you might like to freshen up."

I noticed the basin of water he held and the towels draped over his shoulder as Alton said, "Thank you, that would be most appreciated."

The man nodded and set everything on the table saying, "Daniel mentioned that you had all been on the road a few days, so I thought some warm food would be in order as well."

Alton said, "Thank you for your kindness, I fear I have no way of repaying you."

The man paused in the doorway saying, "There is no need for that. I am just glad to have company in the house again."

Alton replied, "Well, you have our gratitude for whatever it may be worth."

The man smiled politely and said, "Dinner will be ready soon."

Once he left, Luke said, "He is right about one thing, we are a little worse for wear."

I grimaced, looking at the layers of grit on my skin and clothes, thinking nothing short of a waterfall would get me clean at this point. Alton rose and taking one of the towels attempted to scrub some of the grime off. I joined Thomas by the window and peered out into the village around us. I had only glimpsed the castle placed at the far edge of

Carp, but I now understood the name. Even from here, I couldn't help but smell the overwhelming stench of fish. Strange how the Southern Kingdom had been on the water as well but didn't suffer the same fate.

Thomas said, "The circumstances do not allow it, but I think you would enjoy exploring the city. They have an impressive market here like no other."

Alton added, "Merchants come from all over the world to hawk their wares in the market. On any given day you will hear at least six different languages spoken, but somehow trade is not encumbered by the diversity. If anything, it is the reason Carp's market has outgrown our own."

I was surprised to hear Alton speak so highly of another kingdom after showing such pride in his own but I suppose even royals can have humility.

I stepped back, away from the window, and said, "It sounds like an interesting place to visit." Alton replied, "Perhaps you will someday. I am sure Joseph has interests here in Carp as well."

I nodded, noticing Sharrow and Thomas glance over at me. If only they knew just how far I had traveled to come here and the things I had seen. Shrugging it off, I leaned on a small table, not quite ready to sit down again. The last few days had been nothing but hard riding and short breaks for sleep and food. I doubted any of us had said more than five words to each other the whole way.

Stretching my legs, I hoped I never had to

sit in that leather saddle ever again. Maybe we would wrap everything up here, and I could leave. Inwardly scoffing, I knew the likelihood of that happening was slim to none. Then looking at the group, I wasn't sure I was ready to go yet. Something about them made me feel at home somehow like I could just be part of their ragtag band. Then thinking of the family I had chosen to leave behind, I knew I shouldn't waste time wishing for things that would never happen.

"Milady?"

I blinked, looking at Sharrow and asked, "Yes?"

He commented, "You seemed troubled."

Thomas reaching for his sword asked, "Is there danger?"

I shook my head saying, "Not that I can tell."

He nodded, but everyone seemed a bit more on edge.

Sharrow said, "Something troubles you still, milady."

I waved it off saying, "Just a passing thought, nothing more."

He looked at me with concern but let it go. I wanted to explain but what would be the point?

Thomas peered out the window again saying, "The sooner we finish with this, the better."

Alton said, "You must be anxious to return home and see Lana."

Thomas smiled saying, "She is sure it will be a girl this time."

Luke warned, "You are going to have your hands

full, brother. They say girls give the most grief."

Alton agreed saying, "I have heard the same, but at least she will have four uncles happy to help."

Thomas replied, "And I thank you all for it."

Sharrow commented, "We are all looking forward to the newest addition of the family."

The door opened suddenly, and the man stepped in saying, "Dinner is ready."

Luke jumped up and exclaimed, "Finally."

Henry frowned at him, then facing the man said, "He means thank you."

Luke paused and added, "What he said."

Henry rolled his eyes, but everyone else seemingly unsurprised simply followed him out the door.

Chapter 12

We tensed as the door opened and Daniel walked in.

Alton rose saying, "We thought something had gone wrong."

Daniel replied, "My apologies your highness, it took longer than I was expecting to convince Fredrick to speak with you."

Alton asked, "But he will see us?"

Daniel nodded saying, "I am to bring you to him through a back way, thus avoiding the crowds."

Thomas asked, "Does he seem open to stopping the ships?"

Daniel shook his head saying, "No, it is as we feared. Fredrick is no more than a willful child wielding power that he should never have."

Alton replied, "That is discouraging, but we must still try. Our people deserve that much from me."

Everyone gathered their things and quietly slipped outside. It was nearing nightfall now, and I hoped things would go smoothly. If not, trying to find shelter in the city would be impossible.

Daniel beckoned, "This way."

We followed weaving through the streets and staying in a tight formation. I stayed in the back, feeling a growing sense of unease with every step I took. People glanced at us as we passed, but no one questioned it. I guess seven armed strangers trailing through the city was not all that uncommon.

Daniel paused at the edge of a house and looked out at the gate nearby. Knowing in my gut that something was wrong, I reached out grabbing Alton's arm, and he stopped, turning to face me.

I pleaded, "We should rethink this. Something is not right."

Alton replied, "I trust your judgment, Traveler but I must go now. There is not enough time to wait."

I nodded knowing unless I tied him to a post, he was going inside.

Daniel warned, "We must hurry."

Thomas looked from me to Alton and asked, "Are you sure?"

Alton replied, "Yes."

Daniel snapped, "Good; now we must go."

Sharrow looked back at me clearly torn but when Alton dashed across the street, he turned and ran after him. Frowning, I went after them wishing I had just tied Alton to a tree outside of the city instead.

Daniel paused, saying a quick word to the guard at the gate who nodded as we trotted past. Once inside the castle, Daniel kept a steady pace leading us down hallways and up dimly lit stairs marking out a path only he seemed to know. Only a few servants saw us, and most were in so much of a hurry they didn't even look our way. I guess he wasn't kidding about going through the back way.

Shortly after, we slowed and walked into a large room lined with chairs and lit torches. I didn't get the sense that a new king would choose this room for such an important meeting and looked at Daniel in confusion.

Alton asked, "He is meeting us here?"

Daniel nodded saying, "He was very clear about it."

Thomas drew his sword saying, "This is not right."

Alton glanced around the empty room and ordered, "We are leaving now."

We turned towards the door as dozens of footsteps neared, making us race for the door, only to slide to a stop as guards poured in from all sides. We surrounded Alton having retrieved our own various weapons and stood braced for what I knew might be the fight of our lives. I might not be able to die, but I would still bleed all the same.

Alton demanded, "What is this?"

Daniel replied, "I do not understand either, your highness."

Thomas looked at Daniel with suspicion, and I doubted our guide would live long enough for the guards to have their chance at him. Focusing again on one of the guards, I aimed my arrow for a weak spot in his armor but held steady. No one else had spoken, and I had the feeling it wasn't nearly over yet. A single set of footsteps echoed down the hall before a young man wearing ill-fitting expensive clothing dotted with jewelry walked in grinning at us.

Alton asked, "Fredrick, what are you doing?"

The man snapped, "That is King Fredrick to you!"

Alton frowned and offered, "Let us talk as leaders. I know we can find a solution."

Fredrick smiled and asked, "You do not understand what has happened yet, do you?"

When Alton paused, Daniel lowered his sword and stepped past the guards, saying, "I told you it would work."

Fredrick replied, "I was doubtful, but you were right. He followed you right to my door, no less."

Daniel shrugged and said, "They always do."

Alton asked, "You would betray your people, Daniel?"

He replied, "The money was better, and I try to stay with the winning side."

Henry mumbled, "I knew there was something off about you."

Daniel applauded saying, "Congratulations, if only you had figured it out sooner, you might have been spared this next part."

Alton straightened and asked, "What does he speak of?"

Fredrick smug with victory replied, "Oh, just that I am going to keep you all prisoners here, and force your father to give up the kingdom."

Alton countered, "He will never betray his people, not even for me."

Fredrick replied, "You better hope I am right, or you will never see your Southern Kingdom again."

I saw the others sizing up our odds, and they did not look good. I might be able to get Alton out of here, but we would lose most everyone else. Turning, I aimed at Fredrick, and he froze staring at me.

Daniel threatened, "Release your arrow, and you will all die right here, Traveler."

Alton shook his head at me, but I promised, "I can get you to safety."

He replied, "I believe you but at what cost?"

Thomas argued, "No, you will not place us above your people!"

Fredrick shrieked, "Kill her!"

A guard moved closer but Sharrow stepped forward, stopping him with a glare.

Alton ordered, "Stand down, Traveler."

I frowned and stood still a long moment, before laying my bow on the stone floor.

Fredrick swallowed and ordered, "Take them to the dungeon."

A guard replied, "Yes your highness." Then facing us said, "Drop your belongings here."

We set aside everything but the clothes we wore, then were pushed towards the door.

Alton warned, "This will not end well, Fredrick."

Unaffected, the new king replied, "I have already won, Alton. The only thing left is placing my flag over your castle walls."

Thomas asked, "If you were behind this, why send the men to attack us at the Inn?"

Daniel looked at Fredrick saying, "Someone got nervous and sent a bunch of half-wit criminals after us."

Fredrick snapped, "Watch what you say to me, Daniel, there is always room in that cell for one more."

Daniel laughed and replied, "You need me, and you know it. The nobles would never follow you without my nudging them in the right direction."

Fredrick frowned and threatened, "You better prove to be as useful as you claim." Then looking at us, he said, "I hope you enjoy your stay here. Many find the dungeon to be a unique experience." With a decidedly pleased look, he turned and strode down the hallway. Daniel bowed mockingly to Alton, then turned and followed Fredrick. The blunt end of a spear hit my back, forcing me forward and I looked back, glaring at the guard.

Alton said, "I am sorry to have failed you all."

Thomas replied, "You should have let the Traveler take you to safety."

Alton replied, "And leave you all here to die?"

Thomas snapped, "Yes!"

We all paused surprised, and Sharrow said, "In choosing us, you have left your father an impossible decision."

Alton stopped and spun to face him demanding, "What kind of ruler, what kind of man leaves his family behind?"

Thomas countered, "One who hopes to see his people to a peaceful outcome."

The guards pushed us forward, and Alton reasoned, "You would have done the same."

Luke asked, "Thomas is not the prince though, is he?"

When a full-scale argument was about to break

out, I snapped, "Stop it, all of you!"
They fell silent looking sullen, and we walked in
defeat towards our new accommodations.

Chapter 13

The cell door was pulled open, and I saw that it was nothing more than a small stone-lined room with no back wall. We filed inside, and I walked to the edge looking down at the rocks below. They were far enough away that a person would be in more than one piece if they jumped, but I suppose that was the point. The smell of fish here was worse, highlighting our dire predicament.

A figure rose in the cell next to us distracting me, and we all turned as he asked, "Alton?"

Alton stepped closer asking, "Duke Sanford?"

The man reached out grabbing Alton by the shoulders and asked, "What are you doing here of all places?"

Alton sadly replied, "I thought I could talk Fredrick into changing his course."

Duke Sanford shook his head saying, "I am sorry to see you in this terrible place, Alton. I have lost count of how many have jumped to the rocks below."

Alton nodded and straightening asked, "What happened to Theon? Is he here as well?"

Duke Sanford replied, "No, he was sent to Eirian as a bargaining chip. I fear he will join every other who has entered that place and never returned."

Alton frowned and said, "I have come too late."

Sanford assured, "If only there were a way out, I know everyone would fall in line with both of us here. Fredrick was never liked by those in power, and cannot have a strong hold over them."

Alton nodded and I walked back to the edge looking down.

Sharrow stepped forward saying, "Wait."

I replied, "It must be done and you know I must be the one to do it."

He replied, "I do not fear that you will not survive it, milady. I fear for the pain it will cause you."

I smiled at him saying, "Don't worry, I always bounce back."

Alton walked to me asking, "Can you do it, Traveler? I would not ask it if there was any other way."

I replied, "I have never fallen from such a height before, but you won't get back home if I don't try."

Henry promised, "If you can break us out of here, I will take back every distrusting thing I have ever said."

Luke added, "That is a lot."

I sent them a slightly irritated but amused look, and reaching down pulled out a small blade from the inside of my boot.

Duke Sanford warned, "You will never make the climb; it is impossible."

I replied, "We'll see."

I started to climb over the edge when Sharrow said, "Be careful, milady."

I stopped and looked up at him, surprised to see how worried he was and replied, "I will."

He nodded but looked like he would rather attempt the climb himself than let me go. Staring down at the open air below, I shivered a little and started down. Wedging my small blade between the stones, I slowly made my way down.

After going about ten feet, I wished I had one knife for each hand instead of trying to grip the weather-worn edges with the tips of my fingers.
From above Thomas praised, "You are doing well, Traveler."
I wanted to say something witty but instead focused on my limbs that were starting to shake. I didn't know if it was the height or the fact that I wasn't used to climbing, but it didn't bode well for me either way. Despite my brave face, I did not want to find out if I could, in fact, die after all.

Slowly descending, I kept looking up at their now shadowy outlines marking my progress. I could barely see them now in the moonlight, but I guessed all five still sat there watching me. My fingers and one knee were raw where I had slipped causing a terrible cold chill to rush through me before I was able to find a jagged stone to grab. Stopping, I panted thinking how horseback riding didn't really seem that bad now. If I were to see that massive horse I had been stuck with on the way here, I would hug it and be glad to have my feet on the ground once again.
"Traveler?"
I looked up and replied, "I'm okay!"
They went quiet, so I kept going. I had to reach the bottom at some point right?

Just when I was halfway down, I reached for a

new stone to grab onto and heard a scraping sound as my knife slide out, leaving me to scramble for safety. I let out a squeak of surprise and frantically reached for something to stop my free fall but the stones quickly blurred by until I could see only grey. I turned my head trying to see how far I still had to fall as the rushing sensation took over my senses turning the world into a single dark space below me. Then with a flash of sudden pain, there was only blackness.

Chapter 14

I woke engulfed in waves of pain, unable to think. Slowly, the pain moved into specific areas, and I looked to see more than a few bones broken. Dropping my head to the rocks, I felt most of the bones shift painfully back into place before the muscles once again attached, and the torn skin healed, making me the semblance of whole. Then with a steadying breath, I sat up and gripping my arm that stood out at an odd angle, snapped it back into the socket. I cringed and sat still for a moment still reeling from the shock until I realized they were shouting my name. They must not be able to see me anymore.

Standing up I called, "I'm alright!"

They fell silent, and I looked around, glad no one had seen me fall.

Alton asked, "Traveler?"

I called, "I will be there soon!"

I could only imagine what Duke Sanford thought, but it didn't matter now. I had to find a way inside and get everyone out.

Searching the rocks, I found my knife and started for the nearest gate. The time for being careful was long past. My only goal now was getting to the others and getting us all out of this place. Looking up at the towering castle, I wondered how long it would take me to reach them. I didn't think the guards would handle it well when they found out I was gone. Picking up a jog, I headed towards a narrow opening in the wall lit by a single torch. The guard posted at the gate froze surprised to see another soul out here in the dead of night, making it almost easy for me to disarm him. Taking his spear and tucking away my small blade, I left the guard in an unconscious heap on the ground before darting inside the castle. Racing through the chilly halls, I tried to recall every twist and turn we had taken leading to the cells. Upon reaching the room where Daniel had betrayed us, I slid to a stop seeing a servant rounding the corner. Dashing into one of the many shadows, I paused watching the unsuspecting man walk right on by me. Once he passed, I glanced around hearing distant footsteps behind me and raced for the group. I had to get them out before the guard at the gate was discovered. Then remembering my things had been taken, decided I would come back for my bow once the prince was safe.

Finally reaching the doorway of the dungeon, I stopped as five men clad in armor turned to see me. They stared at me with wide-eyed surprise, then snatching up various weapons charged at me with a loud battle-like cry. Gripping the spear I leaped in spinning, blocking, and striking until I was the last one. Then looking to see that no alarm had been raised, I stepped over one of the men and continued going down the long hallway.

Luke who was leaning on the bars of their cell saw

me first and straightened saying, "Looks like you lost that bet, Henry."

The others moved closer seeing me, and everyone began calling out to me at once until Alton ordered, "Silence, you will alert the guards!"

Everyone quieted, and I looked around, eventually spotting a set of keys hanging by the doorway and grabbing them and started towards the cell.

Alton said, "We are very happy to see that you made it here safely, Traveler."

I replied, "I hope Theon is not in a similar cell because I will not be doing that again."

Thomas said, "We could not ask it of you twice, Traveler. That would be dishonorable."

I replied, "If only everyone could be so moral, we would not be in this mess."

On the third key now, I started to wonder if any worked when the lock clicked open and swinging the cell door wide I said, "Finally."

Alton said, "Thank you, Traveler."

I nodded, handing him the keys and said, "Time to replace the king, I think."

Thomas replied, "Agreed."

Sharrow stepped forward with a relieved look and started to reach out to me but let his hand fall away saying, "Milady, you should not have done that."

I looked at the still new blood that stained my torn clothes and replied, "It's alright. There are only scars now, and they are on my back anyway."

He frowned saying, "Still."

Duke Sanford exclaimed, "I do not believe it. How are you here?"

Alton who was unlocking the cell replied, "It is a long story that we do not have time for now."

Once the door was open, Duke Sanford stepped forward, embracing Alton before leaning back and saying, "It is good to see you, boy."

Alton smiled and replied, "And you as well." Then turning serious, he asked, "Which of these men have been brought here since Fredrick took over?"

Sanford replied, "All of them. Anyone who was here before was taken away to who knows where."

Alton nodded and tossed the keys to Luke who started releasing the other prisoners.

Thomas asked, "Who can we trust to help smooth over the change of leadership?"

Sanford replied, "I need to speak with the council. They will have no desire to see Fredrick on the throne a moment longer."

Alton added, "And Daniel must be found."

Thomas commented, "Hopefully he is the only traitor from our lands, but we must find out."

Sanford replied, "Of course, as soon as he is found, I will personally deliver the traitor to you. He will have much to answer for in the days to come."

We started walking as the freed prisoners ran ahead shouting their joy, and Alton asked, "What will become of Fredrick?"

Sanford frowned and replied, "Banishment of some kind, most likely. No matter what he has done, he is still royalty."

Alton nodded, but Henry said, "I think he should live out his days in one of those cells."

Luke added, "That would be more fitting."

Sanford replied, "It will depend on if Theon is still alive."

Alton paused seeing the five fallen guards, and Sanford asked, "Where did you come from milady?"

I replied, "A place far from here."

Sanford added, "If you ever grow tired of Alton here, Carp would be very happy to have you."

I smiled saying, "Thank you but I must see the Southern Kingdom back in order first."

Suddenly, a castle guard came around the corner and seeing us opened his mouth to call out, but Henry asked, "May I?"

I handed him the spear which he threw with perfect aim, dropping the man before he could make a sound. Henry nodded to me as a friend, and I had the feeling I was the only person outside of their group that had ever won his trust.

Thomas warned, "We should hurry before anyone else comes across our path."

I pulled out the spear, wanting to have some form of defense and Luke drug the body out of sight.

Upon returning, Luke asked, "Where would they have put our things?"

Sanford replied, "There is a storage room just down the hall we use for such things."

Henry looked at Alton who gave the go-ahead, so Luke followed Henry checking each room while the rest of us circled Alton and watched for any unwanted surprises.

A short time later Luke, waved from a doorway holding up his sword and we moved that way staying in a tight circle.

Bow in hand and a quiver full of arrows at my back, I was glad to have something familiar once again.

Sanford took the spear saying, "Just in case."

I decided I could see why he and Alton were friends. They could be mistaken for father and son.

Sanford said, "The councilmen should all be in their rooms this time of night, but thankfully they are housed close together."

Alton offered, "Lead the way."

We followed Sanford only passing a few servants who ducked away into the shadows as we neared. I found the castle to be a bit eerie, but maybe it was only like that at night.

Sanford asked, "What will you do once things are settled here?"

Alton replied, "We must locate Theon and bring him back home."

Sanford said, "I will send an escort with you."

Alton replied, "Thank you, but we would prefer to travel as a smaller group."

Sanford commented, "I know Daniel's betrayal was a terrible shock, but not everyone puts their loyalty up for sale."

Alton nodded saying, "True and I trust your judgment, but I trusted Fletcher to provide us with a guide and look how that turned out."

Sanford replied, "I do not blame you for being cautious, and if you really prefer to go alone then I will support it."

Alton assured, "It is in no way a reflection of Carp or its people."

Sanford clapped him on the back saying, "I know that and in your shoes I would likely do the same. You know I am not the kind to take offense so easily."

Alton smiled saying, "Thank you, cousin."

Thomas said, "When the council is gathered, we need to find out about the ships first."

Sanford replied, "I do not believe they have left yet, but I cannot be sure from the limited view of that cell."

I hoped we would be in time to stop them. I didn't want to find out if Carp's ships manned by Eirian's soldiers could break past the defenses of the Southern Kingdom.

Chapter 15

Sanford knocked on the door, and a muffled voice demanded, "Go away."

Sanford rolled his eyes and pushed open the door, leading us inside.

An older man sat up in bed startled until he recognized Sanford, then jumping to the floor with surprising agility asked, "How did you escape?"

Sanford replied, "Prince Alton here came to my aid."

The man froze seeing the prince, and snatching up a robe hastily put it on saying, "My apologies, your grace."

Alton replied, "I think a lack of proper attire can be excused, Councilman."

The man nodded still trying to fully cover his floor length-night gown.

Sanford said, "I am going to take the reins until Theon can be found and I need all the help I can get."

The man almost melted with relief and said, "I am very glad to hear it, Duke Sanford."

Luke who was standing by the door announced, "We have company."

I turned, uncertain why I had not sensed trouble coming and Sanford said, "Time to prove your loyalty, councilman."

Two guards entered and stared at us with confusion before the councilman stepped forward saying, "Duke Sanford, Prince Alton meet Peter and Arthur. They are on our side."

The two guards bowed, and the dark headed one said, "We are very pleased to see you both. Fredrick is quickly bringing everything to ruin."

Sanford nodded and said, "I will repair what I can."

The other man asked, "What can we do?"

Sanford replied, "We are gathering everyone who will help us. I thought it best to meet in one of the main rooms rather than the throne room."

Alton commented, "Yes, I think that would suit the situation well."

The councilman said, "The others will fall in line once they see both of you here. I am sure of it."

Sanford replied, "I hope so."

The light-haired guard said, "We should accompany you until everyone is gathered. Not everyone in the castle is against Fredrick. He has bribed many of the castle guards and most anyone else who could be easily swayed."

Sanford agreed saying, "The more with us, the easier this will go."

Alton asked, "On to the next one then?"

Sanford replied, "Indeed."

We traveled from room to room gathering a crowd as we went until there were nearly twenty following Sanford. With each addition, we feared being attacked even less but worried more about losing time. I could see the first rays of sun reaching into the cold stone fortress marking the new day. In the morning light, I could see how haggard we all looked, and couldn't remember the last time any of us had sat still let alone felt at ease. Maybe now things would be different though.

Sanford opened the door to a large room where an equally large table sat in the middle, leaving just enough room to walk around it. Men started filing in and taking a seat most still in their night-gowns while my group hung back.

Alton turned to Sanford saying, "I will be right there."

Sanford nodded and took a seat not at the head of the table, but in the middle.

Alton faced us saying, "Thomas, if you would not mind staying for the meeting, everyone else can go freshen up and find some food."

Thomas asked, "Are you sure about sending them away?"

Alton asked, "Traveler, do you sense any danger?"

I shook my head saying, "No, but I only have short notice of when it is coming."

Alton said, "That will have to do for now. A runner is being sent after the ships, so you all can take a hard-earned reprieve."

Luke admitted, "It would be nice to put some-thing clean on."

Alton smiled and waving over a servant said, "Please show my friends where they can wash off the road dust."

The man looked at all of us slightly repulsed, but said, "Yes, your grace."

Alton nodded to us then went inside, followed by Thomas.

The man instructed, "This way if you please."
We followed him without a word, everyone too tired to speak as the castle began buzzing with life around us. I wondered if Fredrick knew what was happening and if Daniel would ever be caught. Men like him seemed to always slip away right when you thought you had them. Either way, he would never again be welcomed at any of the places he once called home.

A short time later, the man who had not said more than five words to us stopped and motioned towards an open doorway.
Sharrow said, "Thank you."
The man bowed slightly, then darted off.
Luke said, "I do not think he approved of us."
I couldn't say I blamed him. Henry walked in first, and I paused seeing a large bathhouse. Most of the pools were curtained off, only showing the faintest of shadows behind them.

A young woman trotted up to us saying, "This way."
She sent each of us to a room, promising that someone would be along soon with new clothes. I glanced at mine that was attracting more attention by the minute and happily ducked into the room she pointed to. Setting my bow and satchel on the stone floor, I kicked off my boots and grimaced at the dirt trail I was leaving in my wake.

Hopefully, they would not be too upset with us tracking all over the place. Of course, I had fallen off the side of the castle for this cause so I should be allowed some slack.

Bending down, I tested the water and found it to be wonderfully warm. The servants must stay on their toes to keep the pools so nice. I looked up marveling at the maze of ropes overhead holding the curtains up and wondered when they had come up with the idea.

Nearby, I heard a splash and Luke sighed saying, "I might stay here all day."

Henry replied, "As long as you stay awake. I do not think the servants want to hear you muttering in your sleep."

I smiled, and Sharrow asked, "Milady?"

I replied, "Yes?"

He said, "I know you have already healed, but I worried not hearing any sounds."

Setting aside my quiver of arrows, I said, "Don't worry, I've fared worse, and still come out of it alright."

He was quiet for a moment, and I realized how strange it would be to go back to being on my own.

A soft voice asked, "Milady?"

I replied, "Come in."

The young woman peered, in holding a formal gown and I asked, "That isn't for me, is it?"

The girl said, "I thought you would want something more proper, milady."

Luke laughed saying, "Just bring her the same kind

of clothes we have."

The girl looked at me appearing uncertain, and I said, "Thank you, but he is right. I need something more versatile than a dress."

She looked at me disapprovingly but said, "Yes, milady."

She then left without a second glance. Shaking my head, I decided the next planet had better be set in another time, or Long Feather was going to get an earful from me.

Chapter 16

Walking into the large room, I noted the pallets that had been set out for us in the room originally meant for Alton.

The middle-aged man leading us said, "I hope it is to your liking."

Luke replied, "It is much better than sleeping on the road anyway."

The servant somewhat offended, replied, "I should think so."

Henry raised an eyebrow, but Luke ignoring it walked on past and flopped onto a pallet. Sharrow thanked the man who nodded in response before leaving.

Deciding to explore, I walked into the next room and saw a few small tables with assorted chairs. It was a small but ornately decorated room that I liked instantly. Walking to the single window, I pushed it open and came to regret the decision as the smell of fish flooded in. Hastily pulling it closed again, I moved towards the bookshelf and trailed my fingers along the leather-bound spines. Picking one at random, I slid it out and turned to the first page. The writing was faded but you could tell someone had painstakingly written every word. I turned the pages, not really reading, just passing the time. Then hearing a soft sound, looked to see Sharrow leaning on the doorframe.

He asked, "Catching up on Carp's history of farming?"

I blinked confused then looked down at the book and realized it was in fact completely about farming.

Embarrassed, I replied, "I just like the feel of the pages and looking at the beautiful handwriting."

He asked, "Do you not have books like these in your land?"

I shook my head saying, "Not for a long time." Then putting the book away, asked, "Are you worried about going to Eirian?"

He paused, and his expression closed off, making me wonder just what kind of place his homeland was.

After a moment, he replied, "Yes, I fear what we will find in that place. I never thought I would return after my parents secreted my- my brother and me out of its walls."

I said, "I'm sorry for your loss. I nearly lost my younger sister years ago to a rare illness."

He looked at me surprised and asked, "Someone told you?"

I nodded saying, "I asked Thomas how you all met while we were on the road." Then seeing his pained look, I stepped forward saying, "I'm sorry, I shouldn't have brought it up."

He shook his head saying, "No, Thomas was right to tell you. I do not think of that day often, but it is a part of our history."

Unsure of what to say now, I instead looked towards the closed window, and he asked, "You have a sister?"

Turning back to him, I nodded saying, "Yes, she is twenty years old now."

He asked, "But you have not seen her for some time?"

I replied, "It's been years since I went home. The last time I saw her, she was twelve years old and had just miraculously recovered from her illness. That was the deal though. She would be saved if I spent the rest of my life working for Long Feather."

Sharrow looking confused asked, "The winged creature from myths I heard as a child?"

I smiled saying, "Probably, except he doesn't have wings."

Sharrow asked, "Can you never return home?"

I shrugged saying, "Only if he allows it, and by now I'm not sure what I would do if I could go home. My parents likely think I ran away because I took some clothes and things with me."

He replied, "That is a pity when you have given so much."

I said, "Maybe so, but I get to travel to places most people have never heard of. You would not believe some of the things I have seen. I wouldn't believe it if I didn't see them myself."

He smiled and replied, "I should like to explore new worlds."

I asked, "So you don't think I'm crazy?"

He smiled and replied, "After seeing you heal from every injury, I am more open-minded about things."

I commented, "Long Feather would like you, I think. It takes a while to get past his aloofness but there you have something in common."

Sharrow nodded, and Henry walked in asking, "What are you two talking about?"

Sharrow glanced at me and replied, "We were saying how glad we will be when we can move on from here."

Henry replied, "Yes, I am ready to be back among familiar faces, instead of guessing at everyone's loyalties."

Just then the door opened in the other room, and we all rounded the corner to see Thomas and Alton looking tired but more at ease.

Luke sat up from his sprawled position and asked, "Good news?"

Alton frowned and replied, "Fredrick has been caught, and the ships were stopped."

Henry asked, "Then why do you look as though we lost?"

Thomas added, "Daniel escaped, and we have to find Theon before someone tries to take the throne from Duke Sanford."

Luke asked, "How are we going to do that?"

Alton replied, "At the moment, I have no idea."

Sharrow suggested, "There is a sitting room just through here."

Alton nodded and we all filed in taking a seat.

Henry asked, "How did Daniel escape?"

Alton replied, "He must have found out, and

slipped away in all the chaos."

Luke asked, "But we will find him?"

Alton nodded saying, "Yes, somehow we will find him."

Redirecting the conversation, I asked, "So, how hard is it to get into Eirian?"

Sharrow replied, "Impossible. They do not allow outsiders in for any reason."

Alton said, "But they would let you inside."

Sharrow looked at him sharply and nodded saying, "Yes, I believe they would."

Thomas asked, "What are you thinking?"

Alton replied, "What if Sharrow led us in the front gates? They would welcome the man who brought the prince to their doorstep."

Thomas asked, "And what if they wonder how one man brought all of us there?"

Alton replied, "He will have the Traveler's help as well. Together, they could pull off the ruse. Then we will locate Theon and return him here."

Luke asked, "Oh, if that is all we need to do?"

Henry smiled, and Sharrow said, "I am not sure about this plan. I have not been there for years, so no one will know my face."

Thomas commented, "That might be the only reason this will work. No one there would suspect you."

Alton asked, "Unless you have another plan?"

Sharrow shook his head but didn't look pleased.

Alton asked, "Are we in agreement?"

Luke replied, "Well, it sounds doomed to fail but

you know I am all in."

Henry added, "We both are."

Sharrow nodded, and Thomas responded, "Do you need to ask?"

Alton smiled and said, "Thank you for your trust, I will not let you down. We will leave in the morning after I have spoken to Sanford."

Thomas rose saying, "If that is all for tonight, I am going to get some sleep."

Alton replied, "Yes, all of you should try to rest before we leave in the morning."

Luke walking out said, "That will not be difficult at all. I have not stayed awake this long since Thomas's wedding."

Thomas clapped him on the back saying, "And what a celebration that was."

Henry replied, "It rivaled any royal wedding I have ever seen."

Their voices faded as they walked into the other room and Alton turned to Sharrow saying, "I know this is going to be hard for you going back there, but I can think of no other way."

Sharrow replied, "We must find Theon, so I will set aside my feelings about Eirian for the time being."

Alton nodded and standing looked over at me saying, "Thank you again for everything. If not for you, the kingdom would likely be lost by now."

I replied, "You're welcome, I was happy to help."

He glanced at Sharrow, started to say something then turned and left.

Stretching in the chair, I said, "Luke is right, the

plan does sound crazy, but it might just work."

Sharrow nodded absently and standing I started to leave but seeing the haunted look on his face asked, "Do you want me to sit with you for a while?"

He blinked and rising said, "No milady, but thank you for showing such kindness."

I nodded, surprised I had reached out to him in the first place, but still felt reluctant to leave when he was clearly upset. Then finally deciding he would have to come to terms with this on his own, I quietly started for the door. Just before I rounded the corner, I looked back to see Sharrow sit down once again with a distant expression.

Chapter 17

"We will not forget all you have done for Carp."

Alton replied, "We are allies, I do no less than what is expected."

Duke Sanford smiled and replied, "You are truly your father's son." He clapped Alton on the shoulder and leaning in said, "Do not tarry long, I fear the stability we have built will not last without Theon."

Alton nodded and replied, "We will return as quickly as we can, I promise you that."

Sanford looked at all of us saying, "I wish you the best of luck."

Thomas replied, "Thank you, and you as well."

Sanford looking a little worried said, "Alright, off with you lot."

Alton smiled and turning, swung up onto his horse. I looked out at the various villagers and nobles wondering if Sanford was right to worry. Daniel was still missing, and anyone with the desire to rule could stake a claim. Then looking at Duke Sanford standing there with a determined expression, I decided Carp was in good hands.

Alton took the lead with Thomas followed by Henry and Luke leaving Sharrow and me to take up the rear. We kept a slow pace until passing the gates, then picked up speed. I was not looking forward to the next few days of hard riding, but at least the bathhouse had given us a brief reprieve.

Taking a deep breath, I was glad to find the smell of fish had diminished as we traveled further north. The air grew cooler the more ground we covered but not enough to make me wish I had my coat. Once the sun set, however, I might change my mind.

Ahead, Alton slowed his horse saying, "Time for a short break."

We all stopped and dismounted before tending to the horses.

Taking a moment to hug my mare around the neck, I said, "Never again."

Thomas asked, "Never what again?"

I turned and replied, "When I was climbing down the castle wall I told myself I would hug my horse if I ever saw her again, and never again complain about having to ride."

Luke laughed and said, "Never mind the horse, I would have kissed the ground first thing."

Patting the horses' neck, I replied, "If I hadn't been in such a hurry, I probably would have done that too."

Luke asked, "How did it feel falling from such a height?"

I frowned and replied, "Like I would never reach the end."

Alton commented, "You showed great bravery, Traveler."

I replied, "Thank you."

Henry added, "Sanford was certainly impressed."

I said, "Well, I'm glad it worked because it's not something I want to try again."

Luke asked, "Do you have a number of times you can recover from injuries?"

Starting to feel like I was being interrogated, I replied, "No, it just hurt a lot."

Luke asked, "So you can survive anything then?"

I started to answer, but Sharrow chided, "Leave her be, Luke."

He replied, "I was just asking."

Henry replied, "No, you were having an inquisition."

Luke frowned at him and facing me reluctantly said, "My apologies, Traveler."

I replied, "Don't worry about it, everyone is curious when something unexplained happens."

Alton said, "We should get back on the road, there is much ground to cover yet."

Without a word, we all returned to the horses and started out once again.

Chapter 18

Leaning back on a fallen log, I looked up at the night sky. It was clear tonight, giving a good view of the stars overhead. I shivered a little, surprised at how much the temperature had dropped. Being the only one without a coat, I had sat closest to the fire before it burned itself out. Too bad I couldn't just hop over to my stash of things and grab something. Looking up at the stars again, I knew Long Feather would give me a speech about not being prepared if I asked to return. Deciding to stick with my pride, I kept silent.

"May I join you?"

I turned seeing Thomas in the dim light of the moon and replied, "Sure."

He sat and hesitated a moment, looking uncertain.

I asked, "What's wrong?"

He looked at me and said, "I have a favor to ask of you. Normally, I would never ask for something personal but I need to know."

Not sure what he was after, I replied, "Of course."

He nodded and asked, "Is my wife in good health? Have you sensed anything about her?"

Relieved, I replied, "She is fine, Thomas. I would know if something happened."

He let out a pent-up breath and replied, "Thank you, Traveler."

I nodded and asked, "Why were you so worried?"

He replied, "We had difficulties with my son, and I worry being so far away from her."

Reaching out, I laid my hand on his shoulder saying, "Don't worry, I would tell you if something had happened."

He nodded saying, "I wish there were some way to thank you for all you have done here."

Sitting back I replied, "Honestly, I'm just glad to have a cause I can believe in. Sometimes, the people I am sent to help are beyond saving."

He asked, "What do you do then?"

I replied, "I do what I can, and move on when I am recalled."

Alton sitting across from us said, "I hope you are not recalled yet, Traveler. We have saved many lives by avoiding an all-out war with both kingdoms, but I do not think the worst is over yet."

Sharrow added, "Once we find Theon some normalcy will return."

Luke commented, "We just have to sneak into the most heavily guarded kingdom in the land."

Alton asked, "Sharrow, what do you remember about Eirian?"

We all looked at Sharrow who seemed to pull in on himself before saying, "I only remember pieces; it was such a long time ago."

Alton said, "I know but try to remember the layout inside the walls."

Sharrow stared hard at the ground before him and replied, "The castle is in the center, but the cells are along the walls. Theon will be in one of those cells if he is still alive."

Thomas asked, "how are they guarded?"

Sharrow replied, "There are two guards for each wall since they only have to walk a straight line to see all the prisoners."

Thomas said, "We will need to distract them."

I offered, "I can do that."

Sharrow added, "I will locate the keys and release everyone."

Alton said, "Henry, I want you to stay close by with the horses."

Henry nodded, and Sharrow warned, "If the alarm is raised while we are inside, there will be no escaping Eirian."

Luke replied, "Then we will not allow that to happen."

Everyone was silent for a while until Alton finally said, "There is nothing more we can do tonight, everyone should try to get some rest."

Wordlessly, everyone laid out their bedrolls and settled for the night with a sense of unease hanging over us all.

Chapter 19

Stretching my legs, I walked a short distance, feeling stiff as a board.

Alton announced, "We should arrive by tomorrow night."

I replied, "Best news I've heard all day."

Alton smiled, and Luke commented, "I agree."

I started to say something when I felt a tingling sensation and looking up at the night sky shouted, "No, I'm not ready yet! There is still more for me to do!"

"Milady?"

I looked at Sharrow who raced towards me with a fearful expression as everything vanished, turning into a white tunnel. Shortly after, I was deposited onto the stone floor and straightening, faced Long Feather with an irritated look.

He said, "Do not look at me like that, you have been summoned many times before."

I demanded, "How am I going to explain to them that I vanished into thin air?"

He shrugged and replied, "You will think of something, you always do."

I frowned at him and said, "I meant what I said; I still have more to do."

He tilted his head to the side and asked, "You have grown attached to these people?"

I looked away, and he replied, "You know that is not wise."

I looked back at him and reasoned, "They are good people."

He nodded saying, "Yes they are, but I think there is just the one human you are reluctant to leave behind."

Refusing to answer him, I instead asked, "Why have you brought me back?"

He smiled at my poor attempt to redirect the conversation, and replied, "I just wanted to check in."

I stared at him a moment not sure I believed him but answered, "Things are going well. We have stabilized Carp, and are now on the way to find Theon."

Long Feather nodded saying, "Good, he will be very important in the years to come."

I asked, "Is that why you sent me?"

Long Feather replied, "One of the reasons, yes."

I asked, "What are you planning?"

He smiled and replied, "Nothing that will happen soon, I assure you of that."

I frowned at him wondering if I was doing more harm than good in the long run.

He cautioned, "Be careful in Eirian, many have entered and not returned."

I asked, "Is Theon there?"

Long Feather nodded and replied, "Yes, he is there and unharmed. However, his worth will change once they learn the ships from Carp are not coming."

I said, "Alton thinks we will be there by tomorrow."

Long Feather replied, "You have made good time then."

I asked, "I don't suppose the next planet will have some other form of transportation?"

He smiled and replied, "The next one will be quite different."

I asked, "A good kind of different?"

He replied, "I would think that depends on one's opinion."

Rolling my eyes, I said, "Alright, don't tell me then. At least let me get my coat, it's cold here."

He gestured to the hallway saying, "Of course."

Going around him, I walked down the narrow path lit only by a single torch that never seemed to burn out. Turning to the right, I walked into my home away from home. It wasn't much to look at but served as a quiet place to recover from my various adventures when needed.

Going to the shelves, I picked through the different things I had collected over the years and gathered up a light coat and a change of clothes.

Once I had changed, I paused staring longingly at my bed and promised, "I'll get to spend more than five minutes here one of these days."

Then without another glance, I walked back to Long Feather, feeling refreshed but ready to see the others again.

He said, "I will call on you again in a few days."

I replied, "Maybe not when I'm in the middle of a crowd next time?"

He replied, "The next time I summon you it will

be to send you onto the next planet."

I sent him an exasperated look and asked, "Anything else?"

He shook his head at me and replied, "Not for now."

Suddenly being pulled upward, I braced as I was snatched into the white tunnel then seconds later fell into midair seeing that I was several feet above the ground. Turning, I tried to land in a roll and hitting the ground, barely managed not to land face first.

Looking up at the sky, I snapped, "That was very petty, Long Feather."

He, of course, didn't answer, but the others looked at me with disbelief, their weapons drawn.

I let out a frustrated sound, and Sharrow bent down in front of me asking, "Are you alright, milady?"

I nodded saying, "Yes, I'm fine. Someone just decided to drop me ten feet above the ground instead of just over it."

Sharrow asked, "Long Feather?"

I nodded sitting up, and Alton asked, "Who?"

I replied, "The one who sent me."

Alton asked, "You did not come at Joseph's behest, did you, Traveler?"

I shook my head saying, "No, but I knew you would not believe me if I told you the truth."

Luke asked, "But Sharrow knows something about it?"

Sharrow replied, "It was not my story to tell."

I said, "It's okay, you have all given me your trust, so I can do the same. I was sent here by someone who picked this time and place for me to help. I don't really know why but he is very insistent about finding Theon and returning him home."

Alton asked, "You say time and place, have you been here before?"

I shook my head saying, "No, but I might come back at some point. It just depends on where Long Feather sends me."

Thomas said, "I always knew you did not come from the ocean but asking us to believe this is a little much."

Luke replied, "I know you saw her fall from the sky as well."

Thomas nodded, staring at me with disbelief and I said, "I'm still the same person, I just travel differently than you do."

Luke commented, "No wonder you do not like to travel by horse."

Sharrow held out his hand, pulling me up and I replied, "Well, my way is faster."

Thomas asked, "Do you always appear so high off the ground?"

I frowned and dusting off my clothes, replied, "No, he was mad that I got irritated with him. Normally, it is much smoother."

Alton asked, "What did he say?"

I replied, "He told me Theon is alive but that we need to hurry."

Alton nodded, and Thomas asked, "did he say anything about Eirian?"

I replied, "Only that it is dangerous. Unfortunately, the rest of the conversation was just us arguing about his lack of tact."

Alton smiled and commented, "I can see how vanishing would make things difficult for you."

I replied, "No kidding. What if I had been in a large crowd or riding down the road?"

Sharrow asked, "You are not worried about angering him then?"

I shrugged and asked, "What is he going to do, drop me on a deserted island? On second thought though, that might be kind of nice."

Luke added, "I would go crazy left alone somewhere."

I shrugged and replied, "It would make a nice vacation anyway."

Alton asked, "Do you know when you will be recalled?"

I shook my head saying, "No, and the next time I disappear will be the last time."

He replied, "Then we will make the most of the time we have."

I nodded, and everyone went back to their bedrolls, settling for the night.

Sharrow who still stood nearby said, "I am glad you can stay a little longer, milady."

Remembering what Long Feather said about not getting attached to people, I nodded not quite able to look Sharrow in the eye. When he didn't say anything more; I spotted my things and darted towards them, trying to ignore my feelings about the one person who understood what it meant to not belong anywhere.

Chapter 20

"Ready?"

I glanced over to see the men nod their agreement, each of them looking equally uncertain about this plan.

Alton added, "This will work, it has to."

Thomas assured, "We will find Theon, I know it."

Luke tested the rope Sharrow, and I had used to tie the three of them together, and commented, "I hope so."

Alton looked back at Henry just inside of the tree-line with the horses and said, "Let us be off then."

Sharrow led the way, and I stayed in the back, watching for trouble.

Looking ahead, I saw that the massive walls were a mere stone's throw away. Then seeing the watchtowers and soldiers walking the wall, I wondered if we could pull this off. Sharrow had been right about one thing; if we were found out, there would be no escape for us.

Stopping as we neared the gate, I paused on edge as a guard approached wearily.

He asked, "What is your business here?"

Sharrow replied, "My companion and I have captured Prince Alton and his friends on the road. We thought they might fetch a good price here."

The man walked closer, inspecting us all with cold flat eyes for a long moment then stopped in front of me. He asked, "And where did you come from?"

I frowned at him and replied, "None of your business."

He bristled, starting to yell something when Sharrow asked, "Are you going to buy them or not?"

Alton demanded, "You cannot trade me as cattle! I am the prince of the Southern Kingdom!"

The man frowned at Alton, then looked at all of us again before saying, "Only King Ecgberht will know if they are who you say."

Sharrow appearing irritated, replied, "Then take us to see him so we can be on our way."

Luke looking panicked, dug his heels in saying, "I will not go in there."

Thomas seeing this turned and tried to run, dragging them all with him. The guard frowned at him, and reaching out, grabbed the rope and yanked hard, pulling Thomas off his feet. He crashed to the dirt and Luke barely managed not to do the same. Sharrow started to defend them but stopped at the last second, while I stood perfectly still ready to cut them all loose if things went wrong.

Instead, Alton pulled Thomas back up, and the man turned calling, "Open the gate!" He faced us once again and said, "Lively bunch, bet you will be glad to be rid of them."

I replied, "You have no idea."

He smirked and shortly after the iron gate was opened, and we walked through, scarcely giving the man a second look.

Once inside, Luke quietly said, "That went smoother than I expected."

Sharrow mouthed, "We still have to meet the king."

Serious again, we quieted, and I looked at the large castle ahead placed in the middle of a flat open ground which backed up to a massive mountain.

On either side, cells lined the walls and prisoners called out pleading to be set free. Other than a few torches placed strategically around, the only sign of life was a few dozen soldiers milling around and the clouds of smoke drifting from the mountain. I searched but didn't see a single villager or even hear a barking dog. Chilled, I now understood why Sharrow had dreaded ever returning to this place.

We watched a soldier run ahead through the stone arch and disappear inside. I wondered what kind of reception we would receive from this King of theirs. Would he pay us or decide to throw all of us into the cells instead? At this point, it could go either way.

Sharrow glanced back at all of us, looking closed off and I wished we could just turn back around. Then before I knew it, we were at the arch and reluctantly walked inside. Warm air floated past us heavy with the scent of smoke from the numerous forges giving everything a hazy appearance. The further we walked in, the more stifling the air became no longer swept away by the cold wind outside.

Blinking, I noticed all the servants and castle guards had the same black hair and green eyes as Sharrow. They varied in height and build some, but mostly looked just like Sharrow. I couldn't imagine how strange it must have been for him to grow up in the Southern Kingdom after living here.

Luke seemed to be thinking the same thing as he looked from Sharrow to all the people we passed by. The servants sent us quick glances as they dashed by while the guards stared with open hostility. Moving closer to the others, I kept a firm grip on my bow less certain of our escape plan with every step we took down the bare stone halls.

Finally, we paused at a large opening in the wall marked by a torch on either side and an accompanying guard. Sharrow looked back at all of us and met my gaze for an instant, suddenly afraid. Then turning, he led us in pulling on the rope as Luke drug his heels and Thomas looked around nervously. I had to hand it to them; they could certainly play their roles, even Alton appeared torn between fear and disbelief at being here.

Ahead, I saw a large man sitting on a massive chair that must have been carved from the biggest boulder they could find. It looked very uncomfortable, but then I suppose stone was all you had when your city lived inside a mountain.

Focusing on the man, I noted his seemingly relaxed appearance but sensed he could strike with the speed of a snake if he chose. The more I watched him as we neared, the more he seemed to resemble the mountain its self, covered in hard planes and staring back at us with unflinching eyes. When we were about ten feet away Sharrow stopped, and the king smiled, leaning forward on his throne.

In a deep surprisingly smooth voice he asked, "What have you brought me?"

Sharrow replied, "We captured prince Alton and his two friends on the road a few days ago knowing they would fetch a good price."

The king nodded and asked, "Why have I not heard of you two before? Surely word of an Eirian and a blue-eyed woman working as bounty hunters would have reached my halls."

Sharrow replied, "We have never captured someone high born before, but seeing him scarcely guarded on the road, we could not pass up the chance."

The king smiled and rose, causing the light to reflect off his armor. He walked over to us and looked at Thomas and Luke before coming to a stop in front of Alton. Reaching out, he grabbed Alton by the jaw and leaned his head back, staring at him closely. Alton taken by surprise jerked away but couldn't get out of the king's grip.

Thomas lunged forward ordering, "Release him!"

The king paused and turning to look at Thomas said, "I admire your loyalty, but it will gain you no favors here."

Luke glared at him, but they all stayed quiet.

After a long moment, the king let go and facing Sharrow said, "I would know Charles' family anywhere. They all have those black eyes filled with defiance."

Turning, he motioned to a man standing beside the throne holding a small bag and ordered, "Bring it here."

The man trotted over and handed the bag to the king who then gave it to Sharrow.

He weighed the bag, and the king asked, "I assume you will find enough there to satisfy your companion?"

In response, Sharrow tossed the bag to me, and I caught it opening the bag to see dozens of diamonds.

Looking at them wide-eyed, I closed the bag and replied, "This will do just fine."

The king raised an eyebrow and said, "You must be a long way from your home to have an accent I have not before encountered."

Snapping my mouth shut, I nodded, and he watched me a moment before looking at Sharrow and saying, "You must stay and tell me of your travels. It is so rare to have guests."

I wanted to say that it might be because his home looked like the set of a horror movie but kept quiet. Sharrow almost frowned, knowing if we stayed the night our plan wouldn't work.

As the seconds ticked by, the king grew more suspicious, and I suddenly blurted, "Of course, we will stay. You will allow us to freshen up before dinner I assume?"

The king laughed and replied, "Certainly. I will have someone show you to a room."

Sharrow not missing a beat replied, "Thank you for your hospitality King Ecgberht, it has been a long few days on the road."

The king nodded and looking at Alton said, "You will make a fine prize indeed."

Alton swallowed, trying to look brave and I glanced over at Sharrow, wondering what we would do now.

Chapter 21

I looked back as guards led Alton, Thomas, and Luke away. Sharrow glanced at them, then over at me with a worried expression as we continued, following a servant down the hallway. I shared the sentiment but wasn't sure what could be done about it. This place had more castle guards than Carp and the Southern Kingdom combined. We had to think of something though.

Shortly after, the servant turned down a smaller hallway. This one equally bare but thankfully without anyone else around. Sharrow and I followed close behind the quiet boy who had not spoken a word but only motioned his instructions. It seemed Sharrow had come by his solemn nature honestly.

Coming to a stop, the boy opened the door to a modest-looking room, and stepped back, allowing us to enter.

Sharrow faced him saying, "Thank you."

The boy nodded and started to leave, but Sharrow asked, "Could you do a favor for us?"

The boy looked up at him then and glanced over at me with uncertainty before finally nodding.

Sharrow smiled saying, "Good, all I need is to know where they took those prisoners we brought with us. Can you do that?"

The boy smiled and nodded, then turned taking off at a fast pace.

Once he was gone, I asked, "Are you sure he won't tell anyone?"

Sharrow replied, "The only thing I am certain of is that we need to find them quickly. I do not foresee a dinner with King Ecgberht ending well."

I replied, "Somehow, I don't think he will believe my story about Long Feather."

Sharrow smiled and replied, "Perhaps not."

Turning serious once more, I asked, "Even if the boy shows us the way, how will we reach the main gate once we have the others?"

Sharrow frowned saying, "That will prove to be the most dangerous part, and even if we do not alert the soldiers outside, they will give chase once we are found out."

I asked, "Is there anywhere to hide outside of the walls?"

Sharrow got a distant look for a moment, then focusing on me again replied, "Yes, there are some caves a short distance from the main road. They would afford us a strong vantage point."

I replied, "Good if we can outrun the soldiers long enough that might be our saving grace."

Sharrow nodded and looking at me said, "I need you to promise me something."

I replied, "Anything."

He said, "No matter what happens, you must ensure Alton and Theon escape this place. All we have done will be for naught if they do not return to their rightful places."

Knowing I could never leave one of them behind, I

replied, "I promise."

He responded, "Thank you, I know you will keep them safe."

I insisted, "We will find a way to get everyone home safe, Sharrow; you lot are too stubborn to accept anything less."

He smiled sadly and looking at me said, "I will miss your company and unusual speech, milady."

I paused, reminded that my time here was coming to an end. Meeting his gaze, I replied, "You never know, I may return someday. It isn't uncommon for me to visit the same planet twice, it just might be a few years down the road."

He replied, "Then I will take comfort in that knowledge when you must depart."

Wishing I could stay here forever, I said, "Sharrow-"

Quieting as I saw the boy coming back, I glanced at Sharrow knowing it was probably a good thing the boy returned before I said something that would make leaving even harder.

The boy slid to a stop in front of us and glancing around nervously announced, "I saw them take the prisoners to the row on the left side. They seemed to know the man in the next cell, but I do not know who he was."

Sharrow smiled saying, "Good job."

The boy looked at both of us with a surge of pride and Sharrow turned to me asking, "May I have the payment?"

I blinked confused for a minute then remembering the bag of diamonds in my satchel, quickly handed it to him.

He withdrew a small pile of the roughly cut jewels and handed them to the boy saying, "You must keep these hidden until long after we are gone. Do you understand?"

The boy wide-eyed nodded, then reluctantly pulled his gaze away long enough to look at both of us saying, "Thank you."

Sharrow smiled and said, "You are most welcome, now run along before someone wonders where you disappeared to."

He smiled and pocketing the diamonds turned and darted off.

Sharrow handed the bag back to me saying, "I hope they will do him good and not harm."

I replied, "He is a smart kid; he'll be okay."

Sharrow nodded, watching him go then facing me asked, "Ready?"

I smiled saying, "Always."

Chapter 22

We walked along the hallway and nearing the guards I motioned for Sharrow to wait. He paused curious but waiting to see what I was planning.

Not sure myself, I walked into the hall and seeing the two castle guards, loudly said, "There you are!"

They jumped startled and facing me one asked, "Can I help you with something, milady?"

Ignoring his irritated tone, I replied, "I hope so!" Walking away from the hall where Sharrow waited I added, "They said we would have clean clothes, but no one has come."

Then facing them, I asked, "I can't very well go to dinner with King-" Then pausing I asked, "What's his name again?"

The men looking even more displeased turned following my erratic pattern and Sharrow ghosted by sending me an amused look as he quickly dashed down the main hallway.

Focusing on the two men that appeared to be on the verge of throwing me back into the room I asked, "Well?"

They frowned and the one who had spoken before replied, "His name is King Ecgberht, milady."

I responded, "Yes, that one. It's so hard to keep all their names straight." Then turning towards what I hoped was a path to the back of the castle, I added, "So about those clothes, there must be someone around here who can help me."

The two men soon caught up and the other one I had decided to call thing two instructed, "You cannot wander about the castle, milady."

I looked over at him saying, "I'm a guest of the king, of course, I can walk around."

He bristled and the other one, thing one shook his head stopping whatever thing two was about to do. I kept walking going on about clothes and anything else that would distract them while I neared the mountain. As we went, everyone stopped and came to see what the commotion was about until I had about twenty castle guards and five servants following me, all trying to get me to turn around and go back to my room.

Finally reaching the mountain, I stopped and said, "Well, look at that." Staring at the giant hole cut into the mountain where the hallway led, I asked, "you people really like your stone don't you?"

One of the servants, a young woman, stepped forward replying, "Yes milady, now if you would follow me, I believe I can find you something suitable."

I smiled and replied, "See, I knew there was someone helpful to be found in here."

She nodded glancing at the crowd and said, "This way, milady."

I replied, "Lead the way."

She nodded looking relieved but still slightly fearful of all the castle guards.

Heading back towards the room with my herding party in tow, I hoped I had given Sharrow enough time to reach the others. Now I just had to get past all these people and find a way out.

The woman walked towards the door asking, "Are you sure you do not require my help, milady? The laces on the back are very difficult to reach by one's self."

I tried to look as reassuring as possible while opening the door and saying, "Yes, I will be fine. Thank you."

She glanced over at me with disbelief but replied, "If you change your mind, I will be just down the hall."

I smiled saying, "Thank you."

She stopped halfway out the door and looking around asked, "Begging your pardon, milady, but where is your companion?"

I paused and replied, "Oh, he went to see someone in the village, I think. Said something about family here."

The woman replied, "I see. Will he require suitable garments as well?"

All but pushing her out the door now, I replied, "No, he will be fine. Thanks though!"

She raised an eyebrow but finally stepped out, allowing the door to close.

Letting out a sigh I leaned in and listened to her retreating footsteps. After what seemed hours, I opened the door slowly and hazarded a look down each side of the hall. Towards the left where we had come from, I heard several voices but to the right not a single sound. I started forward when I felt a wave of panic and knowing something had gone wrong with the group, gripped my bow tightly before taking off at a dead run. I followed the sense of panic darting down hallways and through different rooms until I was met with cold wind in the nearly dark courtyard. Spotting several dozen soldiers converging on a small group near the cells, I knew it had to be them.

Reaching back for an arrow I ran towards them hearing their shouting voices mix into a roaring sound with the clashing of metal adding to the madness. Aiming to clear a path for them, I released arrow after arrow until they turned seeing me and the five accompanied by another man dashed for the main gate. I felt a brief sense of relief before half the soldiers started running towards me. Running parallel with the others, I picked off soldiers that got too close to my group, knowing I just had to buy them enough time to escape. Then hearing something to my left, saw rows of more soldiers quickly approaching. I reached back for another arrow but found empty air instead. Frowning, I quickly strapped on my bow and withdrew my short sword as a loud crash echoed across the courtyard. Looking ahead, I saw that the portcullis had been dropped and knew our chances of getting out had just plummeted with it. The group paused seeing this and a mere few feet away now I locked eyes with Thomas who stopped upon seeing me.

I shouted, "Go to the gate!"

He frowned and glanced at the nearing soldiers but pushed everyone towards the gate. Resolved to what I had to do, I spun heading straight into the large band of soldiers. They slammed into me like a solid wall, and I faintly heard Sharrow's voice calling me over all the chaos. Unable to stop now, I ducked, lunged, and spun pushing my way to the watchtower on the right of the portcullis. Distantly, I felt the slice of metal cut through my skin and hoped it wouldn't be enough to stop me. I just had to reach the tower and pull up the gate enough for them to slide underneath it. Then I would worry about not letting them carve me up like a Thanksgiving turkey.

Leaping onto the first step of the tower, I crashed into the stone wall and scrambled up the stairs. Ahead, six sentries stood armed and ready while more came running from the other watchtowers. I heard soldiers climbing up the steps behind me and not knowing what else to do ducked low, slamming into the first sentry and felt him roll over me into the soldiers close behind. Then launching into the others with single-minded drive, I cut a path to the tower only sliding to a stop when I saw the pulley system needed to move the portcullis.

Seeing a flash of color, I looked through an archer's slot in the wall and saw my group with their backs to the gate fighting off the soldiers.

Afraid I might fail them, I turned back to the ropes and pulled each one until the gate groaned inching upward. Pulling with everything I had, I heard the metal groan louder and rise a few inches. Below I saw Alton trying to pull the gate up and yelling for the other man to go through. Knowing there wasn't enough space yet, I pulled harder, but it wasn't enough. Then hearing a shout behind me turned as a sentry, sword in hand, raced for me.

Turning my head, I yelled, "Alton get back!"

Not knowing if he had heard me or not, I let go of the rope and reaching out, grabbed the sentry when he would have run me through and tossed him down the hole. He screamed and grabbed onto the rope giving it the extra weight I needed. Then grabbing it once again, pulled with all the energy I had left. The massive gate slid upward, and I looked to see each one of my group roll under it one by one. Suddenly, the sentry let go causing the gate to slam back down, and I jerked back as the rope scraped painfully across my hands. In the next instant, more soldiers poured in, and I saw that archers were lining up at the wall aiming at what had to be my group below.

Facing the soldiers, I felt my energy draining and knew I would not last much longer. How many days would I spend in this place until Long Feather finally recalled me? Trying to shake the terrifying thought, I braced as the first few crashed into me. They fought with the fury of a hornet's nest while I seemed to dodge each attack with increasing slowness until one clipped me with a shield knocking me into the smooth stone floor. I turned and seeing a sword on its downward arc started to defend myself when the owner suddenly froze and dropped away. They all spun surprised, and I looked to see Sharrow cutting through the knot of men with a fierce grace any swordsman would be envious of.

Once the last man fell, Sharrow rushed to me and bending low said, "I fear we have overstayed our welcome, milady."

I couldn't help the small laugh that escaped and gladly took his offered hand. He pulled me up, and I grimaced feeling stabs of pain that seemed to cover every inch of me. Leaning on him for support, we quickly shuffled out and stopped at the wall. I looked down to see the ten-foot drop below and further out spotted our riding party racing for the trees having left one horse for us.

With grim irony, I said, "So much for not jumping off any more walls."

Sharrow looked back and replied, "we must go now milady."

I nodded, and as one we jumped, falling straight down for an instant, before landing on the ground. Sharrow rolled and rose smoothly, while I splattered like a broken egg. Sitting up, I flinched as arrows dug into the ground around us. Sharrow wrapping an arm around me pulled me up and to our horse that skittered away wide-eyed. Sharrow made a frustrated sound and scooping me up, tossed me onto the horse before swinging up behind me. Picking up the reins, I cued for a run, and the spooked horse bolted after the others. Sharrow fell backward nearly coming off the horse, but grabbed onto me at the last second, managing to stay on.

Feeling myself slipping, I blinked trying to focus as we flew over the ground, heading toward the safety of the woods. Hearing shouting behind us, I glanced back and saw a wall of soldiers flooding out of the gate, thankfully on foot.

Shortly after, we caught up with the others, and Sharrow instructed, "This way!"
I gave him the reins and held on while we raced down the road only to turn sharply to the right soon after, and tear through the woods at a breakneck speed. Leaping over fallen trees and crashing through the far-reaching limbs, I kept my head low and listened to the pounding of our horse's hooves and the soldiers yelling. Suddenly, the last rays of sun cut through the trees, and I looked to see a massive cave opening before us. I thought we would stop, but instead, Sharrow led the horse straight into the darkened cave. We slowed some but kept a fast pace racing along in the pitch black guided by a path only Sharrow seemed to see. I tried to see anything but could not make out even the walls of the cave.

Finally, Sharrow slowed our horse to a stop and breathless, asked, "Is everyone here?"
Alton just behind us replied, "I do not know how

you knew that would work but I thank you all the same."

Luke asked, "Am I the only one who thought we were going to run right into a wall?"

Henry off to the left replied, "Well, it did cross my mind."

I laughed softly, and Thomas asked, "Is Theon alright?"

We all went quiet for a moment, then a voice further back replied, "I am here as well. My horse did not seem to think he should run in the pitch black."

Sharrow leaned forward and asked, "Are you alright, milady?"

I wanted to say that alright was the last word I would use but instead replied, "I will be."

Alton asked, "Now, where do we go?"

Sharrow replied, "We need to follow this tunnel short ways to the opening."

Luke asked, "How did you know how far we could ride?"

Sharrow replied, "I only remembered that the ceiling dropped when the cave floor sloped down."

Luke sounding a little rattled, replied, "Remind me not to ask next time."

Sharrow instructed, "We need to go on foot from here."

He swung down, careful not to jostle me and I started to follow suit when he said, "Milady, you can stay there, just lay flat."

I started to tell him I was fine but feeling my blood-soaked clothes, decided maybe I would stay here for just a little while.

Alton asked, "Theon?"

He replied, "Over here."

I heard them walking around and remembered I had a flashlight in my satchel. Reaching into my bag, I felt the cold metal and withdrew it.

Then facing where I thought everyone was standing, announced, "I'm going to turn on my flashlight so we can see."

Thomas asked, "Will it create smoke?"

I replied, "No, it's not like fire; it's just very bright."

Clicking on the light, I aimed it on the floor first and saw the men jump in surprise.

Alton stepping closer said, "That is most impressive."

I replied, "Normally, I wouldn't use it, but this seemed like a good a time as any."

Turning it briefly so I could see my injuries, I frowned knowing it would be a while before I was back to normal.

Sharrow leaning forward asked, "It does not burn your skin?"

I smiled and replied, "It's perfectly safe." Then handing it to him offered, "Here, give it a try."

He took the flashlight hesitantly, and the others crowded around, curious.

Theon asked, "How did you come by this device, milady?"

Picturing how lost they would all be in a grocery

store, I replied, "I picked it up along the way."

Then carefully leaning forward, lay flat on the horse's back glad for the first time that he was so large.

Nearby, Alton turned to Theon saying, "I apologize for the rough exit, were you injured in the escape?"

Theon replied, "Not at all, and I owe all of you a great debt for rescuing me."

Alton replied, "We would have come sooner, but until we found Duke Sanford no one knew where you were."

Theon asked, "You have been to Carp then? How are things fairing there?"

Alton began filling him in on everything, and Sharrow walked back to me asking, "Milady?"

I replied, "Still here."

He turned and asked, "Luke, hand me the light source."

Luke reluctantly tossed it to him, and I said, "It should last a little while anyway."

He turned and using the flashlight looked at me saying, "Milady, you are losing too much blood."

Knowing I might be pushing my luck on this one, I replied, "It doesn't matter, we have to go."

Alton walked over to me and frowned saying, "She is right Sharrow, we must go."

Sharrow nodded and while handing the flashlight to Alton said, "The opening is straight ahead."

Alton took it and glancing at me said, "We are in your debt once again, Traveler."

I replied, "If Sharrow hadn't come back for me, there wouldn't have been anyone for you to owe, so I'd say we're even."

Alton responded, "Even so, I thank you for everything you have done."

I smiled saying, "I'm just glad it worked."

Thomas stepped forward saying, "Pardon my bluntness, but we should go before they figure out where we went."

Alton nodded and started forward leading his horse. I looked back to see the shadowy figures of the others and knew we would be safe for now at least.

Chapter 23

Hearing a voice in the distance, I focused on it and realized I had drifted off again. Frustrated that I was so badly injured when we all needed to be at our best, and worried I might not bounce back from this one, I looked back at the others and knew I would make the same choice again. If anyone deserved a win at this point, it was the small but tough group I now traveled with.

As if knowing my thoughts, Sharrow glanced over at me with a worried expression, and I tried to look as reassuring as possible while draped over the back of his horse like fresh game.

He started to say something when Theon asked, "How did you know about these caves?"

Sharrow looked away and after a long moment replied, "I hid here with my family years ago when most of the soldiers were sent to the Southern Kingdom. We stayed two days fearing the remaining soldiers would find us before finally leaving because the food had run out."

Theon replied, "I am sorry you went through such a hardship, so many were lost in those days."

Sharrow looked up at the ceiling of the cave and commented, "I never thought I would return to this place, but it seems the caves are serving as a haven once again."

Alton looking over at him said, "I am sorry to have opened old wounds by bringing us here. If there had been any other way, I would have taken it."

Sharrow replied, "Perhaps it was all so I could lead us out twenty years later."

Luke commented, "Either way, I am glad we will not have to fight the entire army."

Thomas added, "We were lucky to escape with as few injuries as we did."

Remembering Sharrow's sudden appearance earlier, I asked, "How did you get inside the watchtower after the gate had been shut?"

Sharrow replied, "I climbed the gate then the top of the wall. They were so busy trying to stop you that they did not see me coming."

I added, "Well you had very good timing, I was definitely on my last leg."

Theon chimed in saying, "Yes I agree, you were all very brave. I am proud to have your family as allies of Carp."

Alton replied, "Standing together will be our only chance if King Ecgberht decides to march south once again when he learns Carp's ships are not on their way."

Theon commented, "He would be mad to try such a thing again, especially without the ships."

Thomas said, "After seeing the way he rules his land, I would not say he is a champion of reason."

Theon shook his head saying, "No, that he is not."

We paused as the tunnel came to an end and moonlight reached towards us as if trying to chase away the darkness.

Just then the flashlight flickered, and Alton said, "I believe the light source is dying."

Trying to keep my voice from sounding so faint I replied, "Push the soft pad on the side."

He found it clicking the flashlight off, and I added, "Just push it again when you need the light on."

He pocketed it replying, "Thank you."

Sharrow led our horse further outside and looking around pointed to a slight impression in the stone saying, "That is our path. It will lead us the long way around back to the main road."

Thomas offered, "Perhaps you should take the lead, Sharrow."

He nodded and turning to me asked, "How are you fairing, milady?"

I replied, "I can tell that the wounds have stopped bleeding, but I don't seem to be healing beyond that."

Sharrow stepped closer with a worried expression asking, "But you will in time recover as before?"

I hesitated, and he took my hand asking, "Milady?"

I replied, "I don't know. I've never charged into a solid wall of soldiers before."

He stared at me looking so genuinely afraid for my sake that I pulled away, reminded that one way or another I would be leaving soon.

Realizing the others were watching, I said, "I'm sure I will be fine, I always bounce back."

Sharrow stared back at me not fooled in the least, then turned and started leading us down the trail.

Silently, we followed Sharrow the only sound

the horse's shod hooves sliding over the stone pathway in the moonlit night. I looked back to see the others with their shoulders slumped heavy from exhaustion but too jumpy to slow down. I hoped the Spartan-like soldiers had turned back for the night but knew the odds were not good. Raising up a little, I turned my focus ahead and saw a divide in the rock. Both paths were lined with high walls and seemed equally ominous.

As we neared, the sensation grew until I called, "Sharrow wait."

He paused and quickly walked to my side asking, "Have your injuries worsened, milady?"

I shook my head saying, "No, but I don't think we should go that way. Something feels off."

Alton stepped forward asking, "Where do they lead?"

Sharrow replied, "The right leads to the road further out, and the left cuts back towards the caves."

Theon close behind added, "Then we should go right, correct?"

Sharrow glanced at me saying, "Yes, if we want to outrun the soldiers."

Thomas further back asked, "Traveler, which way would you choose?"

I replied, "We should go left. I know it will put us closer to the soldiers, but I also know nothing good will come of going right."

Theon asked, "How do you know that, milady?"

I replied, "Just a gut instinct."

He seemed to think on it a moment then said, "You

saved all our lives in Eirian, but I must choose the path that will take us home."

Alton countered, "The Traveler has never led us astray Theon, I believe we should take her advice."

Theon looked at each of us then shaking his head replied, "I cannot agree with you on this, Alton and we are wasting precious time arguing about it."

Alton replied, "In that at least, we can agree." Then turning to Sharrow, he instructed, "Take us to the right."

Sharrow nodded saying, "As you wish." He added, "Mount up, the tunnel is narrow but easy enough for the horses to cross."

In response, I sat up slowly, and Sharrow swung up behind me, gathering the reins in one hand, and loosely wrapping his other arm around my waist.

We started forward, and I looked up at the high stone walls saying, "I hope I am wrong on this one."

Sharrow asked, "Have you ever been wrong before?"

I replied, "Hasn't happened yet."

Sharrow commented, "Either way, we shall find out soon enough."

Chapter 24

Time seemed to drag by as we kept moving along the path waiting to see what would meet us at the other end. I watched the tops of the walls, knowing something was coming our way and hoped it wouldn't find us before we could reach the road once again. If they did find us now, we would be like fish in a barrel.

Hearing something nearby, I tensed looking off to the left and Sharrow quietly asked, "What do you hear?"

I replied, "Not sure yet. Maybe just a bird."

Luke who rode in the back of our line up asked, "Remind me why I drew the short straw? Everyone knows the last rider is always the one who gets hit first."

Henry hissed, "Be silent or the soldiers will happily test your theory."

Luke mumbled something else, but even with the echo of sound in the tunnel, I couldn't tell what he said.

Suddenly bolting upright, I turned and shouted, "Thomas, duck!"

In the next instant, shadowy archers appeared on the walls, raining arrows down on us and Sharrow clapped his heels on the charger's sides, sending him leaping into a panicked race for safety. I heard the others yelling behind us and hoped Thomas was okay.

Keeping low over the horse's neck, I tried to look back but couldn't see a thing in the dark.

Sharrow warned, "Keep your head down!"

I ducked and turning forward again, wished I hadn't let Alton keep the flashlight.

We kept racing through the tunnel hearing the horse's pounding hooves and the fading sounds of the archers chasing us.

Seeing something ahead, I asked, "What is that?"

Sharrow who was still leaning forward trying to shield me replied, "The road!"

I hoped he was right since we seemed to have lost the archers for now. Then mere seconds later the high walls fell away, and without slowing, we turned sharply to the right and thundered down the road. All I could see was the dark road below us and the even darker trees on either side. I wanted to ask Sharrow how he could tell where we were going but didn't think now was the best time to pull over and argue about directions. Instead, I stayed flat over the large horse's neck and kept a tight grip on Sharrow's arm that was wrapped around me. He seemed determined to gallop straight through the night, and I didn't think anyone would disagree after what we had seen in Eirian.

After what seemed like hours of running, I felt that same sense of alarm about Thomas and turning said, "We need to stop."

Sharrow slowed our horse asking, "What do you

see?"

I shook my head saying, "Something is wrong with Thomas."

He turned back, and I looked to see Thomas slumped forward, barely staying on his horse. The others seemed unharmed, and Luke rushed to grab Thomas before he would have slipped off. Alton clicked on the flashlight, and I saw that an arrow had dug its way well into Thomas' back.

Thomas raised up and looking at Luke said, "I suppose your theory was incorrect after all."

Luke replied, "I wish I had been right."

Alton commented, "It does not appear to have done too much damage. I believe we can bandage it here."

Thomas leaning heavily on Luke replied, "Then finish it quickly, we need to keep moving."

Alton said, "The horses are spent. We must stop for a short time at least."

Thomas only nodded in response and Henry dismounted then helped Luke ease Thomas off his horse.

While the three of them moved to the tree line, Alton turned to me asking, "Are we safe for now?"

I replied, "Yes, I believe so."

Theon stepped forward, leading his sweat-drenched horse and asked, "Forgive my abruptness but how could you possibly know that, my lady?"

I started to answer, but Alton cut in saying, "Never mind that, Theon, come and help me with Thomas."

Instead, Theon dug his heels in saying, "I am very grateful for everything you have done, my lady but this is too much to overlook. Princes do not ask strange people from who knows where if we are safe, and I saw the amount of blood you were losing, no one survives that."

Ignoring Sharrow trying to hold me back, I opened my mouth to tell him I could have left him in Eirian when Alton intercepted again saying, "I would consider it a personal favor if you would allow the Traveler the indulgence of keeping her secrets."

Theon glared at Alton for an instant then softened saying, "You are right, of course. It is unforgivable to be so rude to someone who helped rescue me, stranger or not."

Alton smiled saying, "Thank you," and wrapping an arm around Theon, guided him over to the others.

Sharrow who had tensed when Theon confronted me, now relaxed a little before asking, "Your voice sounds stronger, milady, have you recovered some?"

Still feeling like I was half dead, I managed to smile and reply, "I think it might just be the adrenaline talking."

He replied, "I am not familiar with this word."

Relieved I was no longer being interrogated, I deflated and replied, "It means all the excitement helped me focus but it's wearing off now."

He responded with, "Ah, I see." Then straightening

he asked, "Can you sit up a moment while I dismount?"

In answer, I leaned forward, and he quickly swung off before holding both hands out to me. Hearing Thomas groan, I looked to see Alton pulling the arrow out while Luke and Henry held Thomas still.

Seeing that Theon stood just beside them holding the flashlight I frowned, and Sharrow asked, "Milady?"

Blinking I replied, "Sorry," and taking his offered hand, slid down.

Standing, I disliked the wobbling in my legs but felt relieved to be on the ground again. Walking was so underrated.

Sharrow asked, "Is something wrong, milady?"

I shook my head saying, "No, I was just wondering why Long Feather wanted me to save Theon nearly as much as Alton."

Sharrow asked, "What did he say about Theon?"

I replied, "Only that he would be important in the years to come."

Sharrow seemed to think on that a moment as he loosened the saddle then glancing over at Theon replied, "It could be for any number of reasons; he is the ruler of Carp after all."

I nodded and laying my hand on the horse's neck for balance, walked over to the others.

Sharrow offered, "Rest while you can, we must start out once again when Thomas is ready."

I asked, "I don't suppose the soldiers will stop for

the night?"

Sharrow shook his head saying, "They will not stop until we are captured or reach the gates of Carp."

I replied, "Then I guess we better make every second count."

Chapter 25

For what seemed the hundredth time today, I looked back to see if anyone was following us but only saw an open road. The last few days had blurred together into a sequence of riding, walking when the horses were worn out, and scrounging for food. I wasn't even sure how many nights it had been since any of us had sat still, let alone slept for a few minutes. Looking up at the early morning sky, I decided I was going someplace nice after this. Maybe a deserted island or something like that.

"Milady?"

Blinking, I turned in the saddle to look back at Sharrow and asked, "Sorry, what were you saying?"

He sent me a worried expression, looking just as downtrodden as the rest of our riding party then said, "You were mumbling something, milady."

Embarrassed I had spoken out loud without realizing it, I replied, "Oh, sorry, I was thinking about going someplace nice after this."

He asked, "What kind of place?"

I turned forward again and replied, "Nothing too exotic, just something quiet where no one is chasing me, and I'm not living off of roots."

He laughed saying, "Yes, a warm meal would be most welcome."

Luke who had stayed at Thomas' side ever since

the tunnel commented, "That and a soft bed."

Henry added, "I would settle for a chair at the moment."

Thomas who still looked deathly pale said, "You lot sound like a bunch of old men."

Alton laughed saying, "You heard the man, no use in wishing for things we cannot yet have."

Theon who had stayed fairly quiet the last few days added, "We will reach Carp soon and once there, you can all recover from this mad dash across the country. Anything you need, just ask. It is the least I can do after all you have done for Carp."

Alton replied, "Your hospitality is most appreciated, Theon."

Seeing something ahead I leaned forward focusing and let out a relieved sound saying, "Finally."

Theon added, "Home at last." Then looking back at us said, "I know you must be in a hurry to return home but please stay the night and eat a good meal at least."

Alton nodded saying, "Yes, as Sharrow said, that would be most welcome indeed."

Theon smiled and facing ahead once again, happily led the way to the gates. I watched him leaning forward in the saddle, impatient to get home and thought how strange it was that he so closely resembled Thomas. In appearance, they were nearly identical, but that was where the similarities ended. Where Thomas was kind, Theon was distrustful of everyone, especially Sharrow, making the trip seem even longer.

Turning back, I quietly asked, "Does Thomas have family in Carp?"

Sharrow nodded and glancing at Theon replied, "There are rumors that Thomas is Theon's illegitimate half-brother."

Facing Sharrow, I replied, "That sounds complicated."

He lowered his voice again adding, "His mother was visiting her family in Carp many years ago when she went missing. Thomas' father appeared in the Southern Kingdom just over a year later with Thomas, saying that his wife had died while traveling home. No one thought anything about it until people started to notice the two men could be twins."

Shaking my head at the insane story, I replied, "You boys sure keep things interesting."

Sharrow meeting my gaze asked, "Please do not speak of this to anyone, it is a sensitive subject for everyone involved."

I nodded saying, "Don't worry, I will keep his secret safe, and besides, Long Feather is sure to recall me at any moment now that we have found Theon."

Sharrow nodded and seeing the sadness I felt reflected in his eyes, I looked forward again.

"Theon!"

We all turned as Duke Sanford came rushing out

into the courtyard with what looked like half the kingdom behind him.

Theon barely had time to step onto the ground before Duke Sanford pulled him into a bear hug saying, "I thought I would never see you again!"

Theon clapped him on the back saying, "I thought you might like to run the place for a while is all."

Sanford stepped back and glancing around whispered, "I do not know how you do it. I have only been looking after things for a few days, and I feel the need to go tearing off to the nearest cave!"

Theon smiled, and Alton walked up to them saying, "It is good to see you, Duke Sanford."

I turned as someone tried to help Thomas off his horse but Luke shooed him off saying, "Thank you, I will help him."

Turning to Sharrow, I asked, "How long do you think Luke will feel guilty about Thomas getting hurt?"

Sharrow shrugged saying, "Most likely until Thomas has healed from the injury. Luke is not one to take matters seriously unless it is about the five of us."

I nodded and sliding off the large dark-colored horse, patted him on the neck saying, "I don't know who needs a bath more, you or me."

Sharrow smiled and replied, "At this point milady, that is debatable."

Letting out a surprisingly loud laugh, I asked, "Why Sharrow, is that sarcasm I hear?"

He raised his eyebrows and replied, "I know not

what you speak of, milady."

Shaking my head, I smiled and said, "Come on, let's find this warm food and hospitality I keep hearing about."

We started forward, and I noticed people glancing at Sharrow with distrust, the further inside we went. I wanted to tell them they were wrong but knew it wouldn't really help.

Then a loud voice called out, "There you two are!"

We paused and looked to see Sanford striding our way.

He smiled and clapped Sharrow on the shoulder saying, "Alton tells me you saved the day."

A few people stopped to listen, and Sharrow replied, "Oh...thank you, Duke Sanford."

He replied, "Wish I could do more, but I am very pleased to see you lot again. This place is starting to come together once again, but it will be a long road for us, I fear."

He turned to me and frowning said, "Looks as though you had a rough time of it."

I replied, "You could say that."

He nodded and swinging his arm wide said, "Come, let us find you some clean clothes and a place to relax."

We followed him down the large hallway, and Sharrow asked, "Where are the others? I cannot see them in the crowd."

Sanford replied, "Theon wanted to speak with Alton and the other three are tagging along with Thomas to see the physician. Everyone will regroup in one of the dining rooms later today."

Appeased, Sharrow nodded, and I asked, "Has any-one seen Daniel since we left?"

Sanford frowned saying, "Not a word so far, but we will keep searching."

I replied, "Men like him always seem to resurface eventually; you just have to wait long enough."

Sanford responded, "I agree my lady, he has made too many enemies to stay hidden forever."

Sharrow added, "Let us hope so."

Chapter 26

"Be careful, those archers from Eirian might still be nearby."

Alton turned to Sanford replying, "We will keep a careful watch on the road and make it a short return trip if possible."

Theon who stood next to Sanford now dressed in clothes befitting his stature added, "A messenger was sent to your father last night, but I know he will be pleased to see you once again."

Alton smiled saying, "Yes, I will be very relieved to walk the halls of my home. It has been a long time away."

Theon replied, "A sentiment I can certainly understand."

Thomas settled atop his horse looking pale but more himself after getting a night's rest and added, "Let us hope to hear no more of Eirian for a time at least."

Luke commented, "If we do, maybe we could not bring a guide next go around?"

Alton grimaced saying, "That is a mistake I do not intend to make twice."

Sanford nodded saying, "A hard lesson learned to be sure."

Theon looked up at the mid-morning sun and said, "You should try to gain some distance before the light begins to fade."

Alton nodded and swinging up onto his horse

looked at each of us asking, "Ready?"

We all answered with eagerness more than ready to put this aptly-named castle behind us.

Picking up a fast walk, we rode out of the courtyard and through the large gate to the road.

After a few miles of searching every shadow for a possible surprise attack, Thomas asked, "Perhaps we should pick up our pace for a short time at least."

Alton turned saying, "I did not think it advisable when two of us are still injured."

Thomas stopped his horse halting everyone, and replied, "My arm is in a sling, so I am quite capable of riding, Alton."

He sent Thomas a pleading expression saying, "You cannot blame me for being cautious after we nearly lost you and the Traveler."

Thomas softened and replied, "I do not blame you for anything Alton, no one could, but I worry more for my wife than myself."

Alton nodded and turning back to face me asked, "Does that suit you as well Traveler?"

I replied, "Don't worry about me, I'm good to go."

He smiled and cued his horse forward, all but racing down the road. I looked over at Sharrow who shook his head slightly amused and followed after the homeward-bound prince.

Chapter 27

Laying back on my bedroll, I looked up at the night sky thinking how strange it was to be so far away from home and still have things that reminded me of it.

Henry sitting on my left said, "You seem far away, Traveler."

I looked over at him, a large shadowy outline in the dark and answered the stars always make me think of home."

Sharrow on my right asked, "Do you have anything from your home to carry with you?"

I replied, "No, not anymore but when I was young, my family and I would stay up late watching the stars, so there is that."

Luke commented, "At least you do not have your older brother telling you what to do all the time."

I smiled looking over at Henry who replied, "Someone has to keep an eye on you."

Luke mumbled something in response before flopping back with an exaggerated sigh.

Sharrow commented, "I only have the sword my father carried and-"

When he didn't continue, I sat up saying, "You don't have to say it if you don't want to."

In response, Sharrow bent over picking through his bag and withdrew a small object saying, "This was my brother's. My father began carving it for him in the caves."

Alton quietly said, "You never told us where it came from."

Sharrow nodded and handed it to me saying, "My father promised my brother he would see the sea creatures one day."

Hearing the lingering grief in his voice, I looked down at the small wooden object deciding it felt like a cross between a turtle and a stingray.

I started to hand it back, but Sharrow said, "It is for you, to remember us by."

Swallowing sudden emotion, I replied, "It's too precious, I couldn't-"

He closed my fingers over it saying, "Please, mi-lady."

I nodded saying, "I'll keep it with me always, I promise."

He smiled and replied, "Thank you."

Alton sitting across from me stood, announcing, "I will take first watch."

Henry replied, "Wake me when you are ready to switch out."

Alton responded, "Rest while you can, we have a hard day's ride ahead."

Grimacing at the thought of sitting in the saddle once again, I almost hoped Long Feather would recall me now, almost.

Chapter 28

"A more welcome sight I have ever seen."

Looking over at Alton who seemed relaxed for the first time since we met, I replied, "It's certainly the largest welcoming party I have ever seen."

Alton nodded a wide smile on his face, and I looked ahead at the large crowd gathered in the courtyard. Well, over a hundred people were packed in waiting for us to arrive all with happy expressions. In the middle of the only gap stood King Charles with a look of pure relief watching us ride past the gates into the crowd. Several people spoke amongst themselves, but when Alton dismounted and walked towards his father, a sudden quiet filled the group. Before either man could say a word, King Charles pulled Alton into a bear hug allowed for a short time to be only a proud father. Then leaning back he said, "You have shown yourself to be a bold and wise leader, Alton; the Southern Kingdom will thrive under your reign."

Alton smiled and replied, "Thank you father," then turning to us added, "I could not have done it without my brothers and the Traveler."

Charles smiled, and a figure suddenly burst through the crowd heading straight for Thomas who happily called, "Lana!"

Carefully sliding off his horse, Thomas wrapped her tightly in his arm while keeping the one in the sling tucked in.

A second later, Thomas' son ran forward crashing into Thomas and his mother shouting, "You came home!"

The rest of the crowd quickly rushed forward, asking dozens of questions at once, making me wonder if this was what it was like having a family with a few hundred people to welcome you home.

Looking around, I spotted Luke still on his horse surrounded by several young women who were all trying to speak to him at once. Nearby Henry seemed to be in the same predicament but not looking nearly as comfortable with the attention. Shaking my head with a smile, I searched and saw Alton walking inside speaking to his father with a few others in tow. Then finally spotting Sharrow, I was glad to see many happy faces around him all asking to hear about his adventures. He paused as if knowing I was watching, and turned to meet my gaze with a slightly overwhelmed but greatly relieved expression.

I started to wave when I felt that all too familiar sensation and looking at Sharrow one last time said, "Goodbye."

He paused confused then leaped from his horse calling, "Milady!"

I wanted to reach out but knew he would never get to me in time, and the next instant everything vanished into a white tunnel. Instead of worrying about trying to land feet first, I turned back trying to see just a glimpse of those I left behind but only saw a never-ending white. Shortly after, I dropped onto the smooth stone floor as I had done so many times before only this time a deep sadness caught hold of me that I wasn't sure I would ever shake.

Standing, I saw Long Feather a mere few feet away with his hands folded in front of him. He praised, "You did well, Traveler."

I nodded and he added, "Much better than you have in a while actually. I think this trip was good for you."

All but openly glaring at him I asked, "What is the next planet?"

He raised an eyebrow tilting his head to the side and said, "I warned you not to become attached to those you meet."

Frowning at him I replied, "Sometimes that can't be helped."

He nodded, thinking over something and when he didn't say anything more, I asked, "What is it?"

He replied, "I think you could do with a traveling companion, someone to remind you why this is all so important as the five have done."

I asked, "And who did you have in mind?"

He sent me a condescending look saying, "The Eirian of course. He is good for you."

Feeling a surge of hope I asked, "Really?"

He nodded saying, "I will send you back to ask him, but he must understand that if he agrees he cannot return home. I am not a taxi service after all."

Without hesitation, I replied, "Thank you, I will make sure he understands before deciding."

Long Feather nodded, and I was suddenly pulled back into the tunnel traveling at unknown speeds across the stars, but it still seemed too slow. Then before I could blink, I dropped onto precious dirt and heard the crowd around me shriek with surprise as they scrambled backward.

Straightening, I called, "Sharrow?"

People backed further away as I ran trying to find him when he appeared out of the crowd, running to me.

We crashed into each other nearly overcome with joy and Sharrow admitted, "I thought I would never see you again, milady."

I nodded content to just hold onto him for a moment then stepping back said, "I have an offer for you."

He looked back at me confused and asked, "What kind of offer?"

Realizing for the first time that he might say no, I replied, "You can come with me on my travels."

He asked, "Long Feather will allow me to accompany you?"

I nodded saying, "But if you come with me you cannot ever come back home."

He paused and knowing I had lost him; I backed away saying, "I'm sorry, I shouldn't ask you to leave your family. It wouldn't be fair of me to do."

Looking up, I started to tell Long Feather to bring me back when Sharrow reached forward taking both my hands in his saying, "I would be honored to go with you, milady."

Surprised I asked, "Are you sure?"

He nodded and looked back at Alton, Thomas, Henry, and Luke and said, "Can you forgive me for leaving at such a time?"

Alton walked forward laying his hand on Sharrow's shoulder saying, "You must go where your heart tells you to go, and we will always be here if you should return."

Sharrow nodded a grateful smile on his face and the others stepped forward all saying goodbye in their own way.

After they all stepped back, I asked, "Is there anything you want to bring?"

He shook his head saying, "I have everything I need right here."

Alton said, "I almost forgot."

Turning, I looked to see that he held the flashlight and replied, "Oh right, that might have changed a few things."

Alton handed it to me saying, "Take care of my brother, Traveler; he is very important to us."

I replied, "Don't worry, I'll keep him safe."

Alton nodded and looking at Sharrow, I warned, "When we go, you're going to feel like your falling but try to land on your feet and don't let go."

He replied, "I must admit the thought of traveling across the skies is a little daunting."

I smiled reassuringly and said, "Don't worry, it's not bad once you get used to it."

He replied, "I trust you, milady."

Looking at the group once again, I hoped we could

return someday.

Then turning my gaze to the sky said, "We're ready."

Sharrow flinched as we were pulled up and into the white tunnel. Gripping my hands tightly, he watched with awe as we were swept away into the seemingly endless tunnel then shortly after dropped onto smooth stone. Sharrow braced, landing perfectly but looked a little green in the face.

I asked, "You okay?"

He nodded swallowing and looked around at the large room.

Spotting Long Feather approaching, I said, "Thank you for this."

He nodded, and Sharrow turned seeing him with surprise.

Long Feather asked, "Not what you expected?"

Embarrassed, Sharrow replied, "Please forgive my staring, we were always told tales of a great winged creature."

Long Feather sent him a wry smile saying, "People always interpret the stories incorrectly. One does not require wings to cross the stars."

Sharrow looked around the room again saying, "No, I suppose not."

I asked, "Since he is going to travel with me, he should have the same abilities that I do."

Long Feather frowned saying, "Do you have any idea how draining it is to keep you alive? Even I have limits, Traveler."

I countered, "He must have some help."

Long Feather eyed Sharrow for a moment then said, "I will give you both the ability to speak with one another over great distances; that should help."

I asked, "What if he is injured?"

Long Feather replied, "Then I suppose he will have to be careful."

Knowing I wasn't going to gain any more ground with him, I replied, "Alright."

Sharrow said, "Thank you, Long Feather."

He nodded, and I added, "Since you had such a trying last few weeks, I think we should have a vacation."

Long Feather raised an eyebrow asking, "Oh?"

I nodded saying, "Just a few days; that way you can recharge, and Sharrow can grow a little more accustomed to it before you throw us into the next planet that needs saving."

He seemed to think it over, and I added, "I'm sure whoever needs our help will still be there in a few days."

Sharrow glanced at me then back to Long Feather, waiting silently.

After a drawn-out few minutes, Long Feather replied, "Perhaps that would be acceptable. I do not want you to show up unprepared for the next place I have picked out."

Ignoring the feeling I should ask what he meant by that, I replied, "Great! I will go pack us some clothes. There must be something Sharrow can swim in that doesn't weigh a ton."

Long Feather nodded, and Sharrow asked, "Do you need help, milady?"

I shook my head saying, "You're still looking a little green, so just stay put and find your sea legs."

He sent me a confused expression but stayed put, so I headed for the storage room, hoping to find something that would work.

"Milady?"

I looked back to see Sharrow walking into my home away from home, and seeing the distressed look on his face asked, "What happened? Did Long Feather say something?"

He blinked and focusing on me, replied, "He told me that had I stayed, I would have been attacked by a small mob in the streets a few days from now."

Frowning, I replied, "He shouldn't have said that."

Sharrow shook his head saying, "No, I am glad to know I escaped such a fate."

Not having any words of comfort for him, I tossed him the shorts I had found saying, "These should fit."

He looked at them like they were an alien life form, and unable to help the laugh that slipped out I said, "They won't bite you."

He smiled sheepishly, and I added, "Now try not to die of shock when you see my two-piece alright?"

He frowned asking, "Two pieces of what, milady?"

Shaking my head at him, I replied, "You'll see."

He seemed to reserve judgment for now, and looked around the room asking, "This is your home?"

Slinging the bag of clothes and sandals over my shoulder, I replied, "Yep, this is where I keep the odds and ends I find. You'll have a room too; there are dozens to choose from, but most look pretty much like this one."

He followed me out and down the hall to Long Feather.

Upon reaching him, I asked, "Did you have to tell him about the mob? It hardly matters now."

Long Feather smiled a little and replied, "A person has the right to know a thing like that."

Frowning at him, I said, "I think you were just trying to make him feel like he owes you now."

Long Feather shrugged and asked, "Are you ready to go?"

I nodded and facing Sharrow said, "White sand and blue water, here we come."

ABOUT THE AUTHOR

Jordan Kelley

Jordan Kelley was born in Texas and has lived there most of her life. She was homeschooled as a child and is an entrepreneur at heart, having started her own business training horses at just 13 years of age.

In her spare time, Jordan enjoys taking off on road trips, going to the movies and swimming.

For more information stop by jordankelleybooks.com